"And you, what are you called to?"

Ryder shook his head. "I don't know. I used to think…" He passed a hand over his heart. "Well, I've been wondering if it should be about raising and training horses. Maybe what I should really be thinking about is rescuing."

Blinking, Jeri gasped, "Rescuing horses?"

He nodded. "I hate the idea of any animal being put down because no one can be bothered with it anymore."

When the time for Dovie to retire had approached, Jeri had begun dreaming about a way to keep the mare. She'd reasoned that if she could raise and train just one superior horse, she'd gain enough of a reputation to expand.

What if she could actually make it happen, though? And what if she could do it without buying land? Loco Man Ranch was enormous. There ought to be a part of it that could be set aside for horses.

Then she and Ryder could…

She shook her head. Even imagining a partnership with Ryder Smith was ludicrous. Insane.

Dangerous.

Arlene James has been publishing steadily for nearly four decades and is a charter member of RWA. She is married to an acclaimed artist, and together they have traveled extensively. After growing up in Oklahoma, Arlene lived thirty-four years in Texas and now abides in beautiful northwest Arkansas, near two of the world's three loveliest, smartest, most talented granddaughters. She is heavily involved in her family, church and community.

Books by Arlene James

Love Inspired

Three Brothers Ranch

The Rancher's Answered Prayer
Rancher to the Rescue
Winning the Rancher's Heart

The Prodigal Ranch

The Rancher's Homecoming
Her Single Dad Hero
Her Cowboy Boss

Chatam House

Building a Perfect Match
His Ideal Match
The Bachelor Meets His Match
The Doctor's Perfect Match

Visit the Author Profile page at Harlequin.com for more titles.

Winning the Rancher's Heart

Arlene James

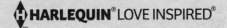

H HARLEQUIN® LOVE INSPIRED®

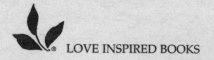

Recycling programs
for this product may
not exist in your area.

LOVE INSPIRED BOOKS

ISBN-13: 978-1-335-47922-8

Winning the Rancher's Heart

www.Harlequin.com

Printed in U.S.A.

And when ye stand praying, forgive, if ye have ought against any: that your Father also which is in heaven may forgive you your trespasses.
—*Mark* 11:25

My thanks to Tyree Rather Brown
for her help with the research on this book.

Any mistakes are my own
and not a result of her counsel.

Keep that cowgirl life going, Tyree.
We love you.

DAR

Chapter One

Folding up the collar of his insulated, sherpa-lined denim coat, Ryder pulled the door of the big barn shut and lifted his shoulders in an attempt to close the gap between the brim of his black felt hat and the edge of his woolly collar. It was the cowboy's lot to freeze his ears in winter and burn his skin in summer, but neither the summers he and his brothers had spent at Loco Man Ranch nor a childhood in his native Houston had prepared Ryder Smith for an Oklahoma winter. An impending ice storm to bring in the new year was just one of the unusual weather events he'd experienced since he and his brothers had taken up permanent residence on the two-thousand-acre ranch they'd inherited from their late uncle. Still, in the past nine months, Ryder had found ranch life more to his liking than he'd expected, especially when it came to the horses.

His guilt at having been the initial cause of this move from Houston to Oklahoma had waned as his older brothers had both found wives and established their own families. Wyatt and Jake were happy, and that helped, but a mountain of guilt remained.

Taking comfort from the whickers and thumps of the feeding horses tucked into their cozy stalls, Ryder pushed away thoughts of guilt and tragedy as he set out through the cold of early January toward the recently remodeled old ranch house. While the ranch belonged to the Smith brothers, the ranch house had been inherited by their late uncle's stepdaughter, Tina, who had intended from the beginning to turn the place into a bed-and-breakfast. As Tina was now his sister-in-law, that was not as much of a problem as Ryder had feared it would be.

His oldest brother, Wyatt, plus Tina and Tina's seven-year-old son, Tyler, occupied the house. Jake, the middle Smith brother, along with his new wife, Kathryn, and his son, Frankie, now four, lived in War Bonnet, the small town just to the west of the ranch. That left the modest, remodeled bunkhouse as Ryder's private domain, though he took his meals in the kitchen of the main house with the family.

Drawing near the expansive carport, Ryder saw that two of the extra bays were filled with pickup trucks. One, a double-cab dualie, he recognized as that of their good friend and nearest neighbor, Stark Burns, the local veterinarian. The other, also a double-cab with dual rear wheels, bore Texas plates and looked brand-new, despite the mud and dust insulting its shiny black paint.

Ryder had been thinking about buying his own truck, but they already had half a dozen vehicles on the ranch, including two trucks, Tina's hulking SUV, two ATVs and the little sedan his sister-in-law had brought with her from Kansas, which had been given over to him. He appreciated the gesture, but at six feet three inches and 225 pounds, he found the compact car a tight, un-comfortable fit.

Deliberately walking between Stark's truck and the black dualie, Ryder took careful stock of the new vehicle. When he spied the chrome emblem just above the wheel well next to the driver's door, he stopped. He'd seen that emblem before, on the rodeo prize trucks exhibited at the Houston Livestock Show and Rodeo. That event wasn't scheduled until the end of March, but the national rodeo finals had taken place in Las Vegas less than a month ago. Looked like they had some sort of rodeo royalty visiting.

Ryder took the steps up to the backdoor stoop in two long strides and let himself into the warm, fragrant kitchen that was the heart of the house. Jake's wife, Kathryn, rolled out a piecrust on the stainless-steel island. As expected, Wyatt and two others sat hunched over coffee cups at the rectangular wrought-iron table at the back of the large, completely remodeled kitchen, while Wyatt's wife, Tina, relaxed in her chair, her hands folded over her distended belly. The shock of her pregnancy coming so soon after their wedding had given way to the shock of learning she was carrying twins. Ryder couldn't help worrying about her, but at the moment his attention was focused on the others at the table.

One of the visitors was indeed Stark Burns, whose long, lanky frame could not be mistaken. The other was markedly more petite and shapely, with long dark hair flowing down her back from beneath a brown felt hat with the tall, pinched crown and sharply folded brim of what was known as the rodeo crease. The hat was a little ornate for daily wear, the brim being underlaid with silver lace, but then the wearer was rather ornate herself.

All heads turned as Ryder closed the door against the cold weather and automatically reached up to remove his own hat, but the face beneath that silver lace arrested his movement. Round eyes almost as dark as his own regarded him from beneath slender brows with the barest arch. A small, straight nose, apple cheeks, pale pink lips and a chin that managed to be both pointed and squared-off at the tip in an otherwise oval face completed the picture. Dressed all in brown, she was young and stunningly beautiful.

Ryder managed to get his hat off his head and onto one of a row of pegs mounted on the wall next to the door, but he had a little trouble getting out of his coat, his gaze constantly flying back to the beauty at the table. When he finally hung the coat next to his hat, he could only pray that the collar of his long-sleeved flannel shirt and the white thermal shirt beneath it disguised the flush burning up from the center of his chest. Nodding in silent greeting, he turned toward the coffeepot. Tina called to him from the table.

"Ryder, say hello to our new guest."

He pulled down a coffee mug from the cabinet and turned to nod again. This time, he added a friendly, casual, slightly disinterested smile. Meanwhile, his heart beat like a big bass drum. He'd never seen anything like her, not in real life.

"Hello."

"Hello."

"Jeri, this is Wyatt's youngest brother," Tina said. "Ryder, this is Jeri Bogman."

Jeri seemed like an oddly masculine name for a supremely feminine woman. It was also a name he thought he might have heard before, but he couldn't quite place it.

"Did you have to break ice for the horses?" Wyatt asked.

Ryder shook his head and turned back to the coffeepot. "Nope. I don't think we're going to need the heating system. The drapes seem to keep the stalls warm enough." Drapes, in this case, consisted of thick, insulated plastic sheets that closed off the horse stalls from the rest of the cavernous barn.

With his pregnant sister-in-law absorbed by her son, her coming twins and her B and B, Wyatt managing the cattle, sod production and mineral leases, and Jake busy with his family and auto repair shop, Ryder had fallen into place on the ranch as general handyman and horse wrangler. It wasn't a bad life for a twenty-five-year-old. He would be twenty-six in less than a month, however, which put him more than halfway to thirty, and he couldn't help thinking that he ought to be doing something more.

Once, he'd thought he knew what that something more was, but life had proved him wrong. He was good—actually, he was expert—at several martial arts. But he was not a fighter, and why he'd thought he could be, he didn't know now. He'd also had it in his head to raise horses, but Wyatt was proving surprisingly cautious about such an enterprise.

"You've got seven animals in there," Stark said as Ryder poured coffee into his mug. "The drapes and their body heat should keep them warm enough."

"It's sure warmer in there than outside," Ryder commented, turning back to face the others.

He found Jeri Bogman sitting sideways in her chair, her gaze pinning him in place like a needle through a bug on a specimen board. He had a difficult time widening his gaze to include the others, but he had to look somewhere other than at the dark-haired, dark-eyed beauty at the table. He made himself turn to Kathryn.

"Potpie for lunch, I see. Chicken, pork or beef?"

Kathryn smiled. "Beef, of course. That's what fills our freezer."

"Yum."

"You must join us for meals, Jeri," Tina said. "As you're our only guest just now, you're welcome to join us here at the family table."

That comment drew Ryder's gaze right back to the newcomer. Her stare, still targeted squarely on him, telegraphed some sort of challenge. He had no idea what that might be about, and it made him almost as uncomfortable as his visceral reaction to the woman. Every time he looked at her, he felt frozen, trapped. Enthralled.

"Jeri's boarding four horses with me," Stark said. "We draped their space, too, *and* added heaters."

"No armed guards?" Wyatt quipped. "I'd have a hard time letting horses like that out of my sight."

Jeri turned her head to smile at Wyatt, and Ryder found he could breathe and behave normally again.

"I take it these are registered horses," he commented, struggling not to stare at Jeri Bogman over the rim of his cup. Purebred horses with proven lineage could be registered with various organizations. His ambitions did not reach as high as registered stock. He'd be happy to produce good riding horses, either through trade or a small breeding program, something he could handle on his own.

He sipped hot coffee and leaned back against the counter, only to have Tina wave him over to the table. Wyatt punctuated the silent order with a flat, big-brother glare. Ryder meandered over and took the seat at the end of the table, with Stark on his left and the beautiful Jeri Bogman with the special horses next to Stark. Wyatt sat at the other end with Tina on his left. Her babies weren't due until April, so she still had at least three months to go, but twins made quite a bundle.

"My horses are more than just registered," Jeri informed Ryder in a low, husky alto that sent waves of awareness through him. "They're champion barrel racers. Or will be."

He focused on the dark well of his mug, fighting to maintain his equilibrium. "I saw the emblem on the truck outside. Win that at the National Finals Rodeo?"

She shifted around on her chair and braced her elbows against the tabletop. "No. I won that in Georgia. I only placed second in the national finals."

Only second. That was nothing to sneeze at. "Congratulations," Ryder said, folding his forearms against the tabletop.

"Second place at the NFR is big money," Stark said needlessly. "Which, I venture to say, is why Jeri's here."

"Oh?"

"I'm looking for property," she divulged. "I've established myself well enough to produce and train top-notch racers. The next obvious step is a breeding ranch and training center."

"And she'll be staying with us while she's land shopping," Tina announced happily.

"Sure beats a motel room or the coffin bed in my trailer," Jeri said, smiling.

Ryder wasn't certain how he felt about Jeri Bogman being a semipermanent resident of the War Bonnet area, let alone a permanent one. He didn't like the way she affected him. He seized on the first sensible question that came to mind.

"Why choose our little corner of the world?"

She clasped her coffee cup with small, delicate hands. "I'm still competing and, God willing, will be for many years. This area is fairly centrally located. There's land to be had, and it's relatively inexpensive. Cost of living is reasonable, and there are numerous properties between Duncan and Ardmore and Red River. Most important, it's decent horse country."

Ryder smiled at his big brother. "That's what I've been telling Wyatt. We've got some good horse pasture here."

"And I said I'd consider expanding the operation to include raising horses," Wyatt reminded him.

"So?" Ryder pressed.

"So, I'm considering it."

Stark drained his coffee cup and got up to leave. "Well, I have an appointment. Thanks for the hospitality. Jeri, I'll probably see you when you come over to care for the horses. Hope the property hunt goes well."

Jeri looked up at him and smiled. "Thanks so much." She looked at Tina then, adding, "Because I have a rigorous competition schedule, I'll only have two or three days a week to look around, so this could take a while."

Tina looked decidedly happier about that than Ryder felt. He'd resigned himself to the fact that romantic relationships would not be part of his life, and he surely didn't want to make a fool of himself over this woman. She was young, beautiful and already accomplished enough to be setting up her own horse ranch, while he was hanging here on his brothers' shirttails. In other words, she was out of his league. Besides, he hated to think what her reaction, or any woman's, might be when she discovered he was also an accused murderer.

Wyatt and Tina called out their farewells as Stark threw on his coat, grabbed his hat and went out into the cold. The door barely closed before Wyatt pushed back his chair.

"Ryder, I could use your help haying the cattle and putting out mineral blocks in the southeast section before the storm hits."

The southeast section was too rough to be reached any way except by horseback. Once a week or so for at least a couple of months in winter, they loaded up special sledges with hay and minerals, harnessed the sledges to some horses and hauled everything out to provide extra nutrients to the livestock.

"No problem. But I haven't seen Delgado yet. Reckon he'll be here by the time we're ready to load the horses." Delgado, who lived in town, was their only hired hand.

"We'll have to trail the horses," Wyatt said, "so we'll just tie them onto the back of the trailer. Delgado could haul them in a trailer, but he won't be in today. He mentioned that he needed supplies, so I told him to stay in town and take care of it. Didn't want him getting trapped at home without the necessities if the weather turns off worse than they predict."

Ryder gulped down as much of his coffee as he could before replying. "We better get moving, then, if we're going to finish before lunch."

"You saddle the horses, I'll start loading the trailer with hay."

"I took care of that yesterday afternoon."

"Good job. We'll just have to load the mineral blocks then."

"I can help," Jeri said, looking from one man to the other.

Ryder and Wyatt traded glances. "Oh, we couldn't ask you to," Ryder began, but she cut him off.

"I'm an excellent rider, and I'd welcome the chance to look at your range."

Trying to telegraph refusal to his brother, Ryder tilted his head. Wyatt got the message.

"It's awful cold out there."

She pushed back from the table. "I have warm clothes. Just let me change."

"Thank you, Jeri," Tina said, widening her eyes at Wyatt, who smiled at Jeri.

"Yes. Thank you, Jeri."

"Guess I'll saddle three horses," Ryder muttered, heading for the door. He couldn't help being irritated. The woman disturbed him, made him uncomfortable somehow. And yet, when he thought back to the first instant he'd laid eyes on her, he couldn't help smiling. Beautiful and accomplished. What man in his right mind wouldn't want to spend the morning with that? All he had to do was remind himself that nothing could come of it.

As if he could forget.

Jeri dropped her favorite hat on the dresser and threw open the suitcase atop the pretty mauve bedspread. Needing to appear the prosperous potential landowner, she'd dressed with a purpose today—but now she could put on the clothes in which she felt most at home. Quickly pulling out worn jeans and a pair of long-sleeved thermal tops, she sat on the edge of the tall bed to yank off her boots, her mind working busily over all that had led her to this point.

She couldn't help wishing that he wasn't so good-looking. She'd known, of course, that Ryder Smith was a big, fit hulk of a man with coal black hair. She'd seen the tape of the sparring workout with her brother, as well as promotional photos of him in various fighting poses. Besides, she'd caught glimpses of him on Houston's local television news. That hadn't quite prepared her for the live version, however. He was meant to look fierce and brutal in the publicity pictures, and he'd kept his head down and face averted during much of the media snippets. In the one interview that he'd done immediately after the incident, he'd had crocodile tears streaming down his face, and that had so appalled and infuriated Jeri that she hadn't been able to see anything but his obviously phony emotion. Coming face-to-face with the real deal today had momentarily stunned her, and she knew she'd stared like a giddy groupie when he'd first entered the house.

Quickly slipping on pink thermals and faded denim, she mulled over that video of the sparring match that had ended with her beloved little brother's death. The video, taped by Smith's manager, conveniently did not show Ryder Smith actually killing Bryan; yet, the Houston police had used it to exonerate Smith of any wrongdoing in her brother's death. After watching that tape repeatedly, she'd thought she was prepared to meet in person her baby brother's murderer, but she hadn't expected soft, shy eyes so dark a brown they were almost black, or a boyish smile that contrasted decidedly with the dark shadow of his beard and the heavy slashes of his eyebrows. If not for the broadening of the bridge of a nose that had been broken at least once, he would be devastatingly handsome. Even knowing what she knew about him, she couldn't deny that he was the type to make hearts flutter.

The sheer size of him told her that he'd continued to use steroids despite having left the fight cage. Even under multiple layers, the hard bulge of toned muscles showed. In fact, he looked even bigger and more muscular now than he had in the tape. No doubt he could break her in two without even trying, but she wouldn't let that intimidate her. If she could handle a half ton of spirited stud horse, she could handle one good-looking steroid freak for long enough to see him held accountable for what he'd done. After all, it was not like she had much choice in the matter.

Her mother had not known a moment's peace since Bryan's death, and Dena Averrett had suffered enough. Her mom had been orphaned at an early age and grown up in foster care. Jeri's father had fallen off a construction scaffold and died when Jeri was a newborn. Then her stepfather, who had treated Jeri as his very own even after Bryan had arrived, had succumbed suddenly to an undetected heart condition almost six years ago. Bryan had become the man of the family at only seventeen. It simply wasn't fair that he had died so soon after his twenty-first birthday.

Jeri had relished the role of big sister, and Bryan had always been her number one supporter in all that she did. But while she'd loved and cherished her brother, he had been their mother's whole world. His death had been a devastating blow, one she feared her mother would never recover from. Unless Jeri could give her some closure by bringing his killer to justice.

As Jeri pulled on her comfortable work boots, she reflected bitterly that the police hadn't even tried to build a case against Ryder Smith, despite the suspicious circumstances. Jeri and her mother felt certain she'd find evidence of steroid abuse by Ryder Smith to bolster their suspicions. Surely that would be enough to force the police to take action. It was well known, after all, that steroid use was rampant among bodybuilders and mixed martial arts fighters.

The police maintained that she and her mother were not entitled to see the results of toxicology tests Smith had taken right after the incident. If Smith hadn't tested positive for steroids, though, why had he left the business immediately after the tests? After all, he was being touted as the most skilled challenger to enter the cage since MMA had become popular.

She and Dena had tried to prove their point via the press in Houston by feeding the media monster bits of supposition, suspicion and facts through anonymous sources and lawyers. They'd managed to steer the coverage away from themselves and shine a glaring spotlight on Ryder Smith, but they'd also driven him and his brothers out of town. It had taken months and a good deal of money to find out where they'd gone. Jeri had competed relentlessly to gain the necessary funds.

The effort had paid off in more than one way, however. She'd honed her craft and earned her way, at just twenty-four years of age, to the national rodeo finals this past December, where she'd won enough prize money to put this last, desperate plan into motion. If everything went well, she was going to prove that Ryder Smith had killed her brother in a fit of rage induced by the illegal use of steroids.

Failing that, she'd see him punished for drug use.

As a last resort, if all else failed, she'd provoke him into attacking her and press charges against him. She'd find *some* way to land Ryder Smith in jail, where he belonged.

No matter how breathtakingly handsome he was.

Then maybe she and her mom could find a modicum of peace.

Chapter Two

Stepping over the high threshold in the small door cut into the front of the enormous old barn, Jeri paused to allow her eyes to adjust to the gloom. She walked down a wide aisle beneath the slanted roof, pausing to poke her head into a well-organized tack room. Everything seemed of good quality but utilitarian. She owned thousands of dollars' worth of fancy tack, most of which she'd won, but like most serious riders and trainers, Jeri preferred simple, top-quality tack for everyday work. It seemed that someone at Loco Man Ranch thought the same way.

Through a wide-open space straight across from the tack room, she could see into the empty cavern of the center section of the barn. What she could see of a third section on the far side of the mammoth structure seemed to contain rooms and storage bins, with an old-fashioned hayrick above. Two doors, closed against the cold, filled the exterior wall at the front of the center section. A heavy, insulated curtain of cloudy, translucent plastic hung across the aisle just past the tack room, stretching to the nearest interior wall.

She heard a deep, warm, masculine voice speaking from behind the insulating drape.

"Steady on, girl. You wouldn't be so anxious to get out of this stall if you knew how cold it is out there."

In reply, a horse snuffled and clopped as it shifted its weight. Jeri thrust her arms through the slit in the drape and parted it just wide enough to slip through. The dirt floor of the stable aisle had been deeply raked and amply sanded with sawdust, but the stalls had been matted with rubber and overlaid with chopped flax. Impressed at the level of care, she looked into the first stall, where a tall, silver gray roan stood saddled and chewing its bit.

She moved on to the next stall, where she found a big red dun with a white blaze on its forehead. It, too, had been saddled. Across the way, she found a fat white pony with brown splotches, then two standard brown bays, both of good conformation but unremarkable, followed by an unusually colored gelding. Its coat, sort of a mousy gray-brown, was too dark for it to be a buckskin but lighter than that of a standard bay—a distinctive animal. Finally, in the next to the last stall, she came upon Ryder Smith tightening the saddle girth of an exquisite copper Perlino. Its pale gold coat seemed to pick up a pinkish glow from the fiery copper mane and tail.

"That's a beauty," Jeri said, hanging over the sliding, metal pipe gate.

"Yep."

Obviously, he'd known she was coming, probably tracking her progress by the subtle shifts, blows and rumbles of the horses. This was a man who knew his animals. She tried not to like that about him.

Without so much as a glance in her direction, Ryder

stooped to push a shoulder into the horse's side, forcing it to release air as he tightened the girth. He had removed his gloves to keep them from getting caught in the straps. They hung from the back pocket of his jeans. Jeri snatched her gaze away, focusing on the mare.

"What's her name?"

"Pearl."

"Apt, very apt, given the lustrous quality of that coat. Is she fast?"

"Not particularly. She's Tina's horse, but she's not been getting much exercise lately, so I thought we'd take her out."

Jeri hated to disparage her hostess, but she wanted, needed, to poke at Ryder, see just how touchy he might be—and remind herself that she wasn't there to stare at handsome cowboys.

"Hmm. Well, lots of people can't be bothered to ride in the cold."

He chuckled, the sound a mere rasp of air. "You might've noticed that Tina's pregnant."

"Sure. But I've known lots of pregnant women who rode right up to their last month."

He spared her a glance then, one thick brow slightly arched, his smile a little crooked. "Were any of them carrying twins?"

"Twins," Jeri echoed, surprised. "I don't think I've ever known anyone who's had twins."

"Come to that, I don't guess I have, either." He finished tucking the end of the girth and let down the stirrups. A horn tooted outside. Ryder wrapped the ends of the reins around a hook in a recess of the wall and turned to open the stall gate.

Instead of moving, Jeri just stood there, meeting

his gaze, her hands clasped around the top rung of the metal. He tilted his head slightly, as if trying to figure out what she was doing. The corner of his mouth quirked before widening into a lopsided smile. After a few moments, the horn sounded again.

"That'll be Wyatt," he said, the soft rumble of his deep voice washing over her in waves. "Excuse me."

Jeri stepped back, perplexed and a little shaken. He was not the irritable, antsy, steroid-fueled maniac she'd expected. In fact, he seemed a quiet sort, gentle despite his obvious strength. And much, much too attractive.

He slid the gate open far enough to move through it, stepped around her and strode toward the front of the barn. She watched until he pushed through the slit in the drape. Only after the heavy plastic of the drape clacked and rustled together behind him did she even think to move. Stepping into the stall, she introduced herself to Pearl, blowing softly into the Perlino's nostrils and gently rubbing between them. Then she pivoted and quickly followed Smith from the enclosure.

She heard the creaks and groans of the great doors as they opened, accompanied by blustery swirls of cold air and an influx of gray light. The sound of an engine followed. Jeri came around the end of the wall to see Ryder motioning a big bronze-colored dualie toward a flatbed trailer stacked with bales of hay. Wyatt got the truck positioned to mate the hitch and joined his younger brother at the trailer, nudging Ryder out of the way.

"I'll take care of this if you'll grab half a dozen salt blocks and put them in the bed of the truck."

"Will do."

Ryder disappeared into a room in the third section of the barn. Jeri trotted after him and got there just in time to meet him as he carried a fifty-pound block of salt mixed with other necessary minerals through the door.

"Here, let me take that," she said.

"It's heavy."

"I carry them all the time."

He didn't argue. "Okay."

Out of habit, she pushed back her sleeves and made a cradle of her arms. Stepping close, he carefully shifted the block into her arms. The unexpected warmth of his bare hands against the chilled flesh of her inner wrists shocked her. She dropped the block, which hit his left foot. Yelping, he yanked back, grimacing in pain. She braced herself for an explosion, but his only reaction was to gasp in a steadying breath, place his injured foot flat on the floor as if testing it and then shake his head.

She couldn't stop her apology. "I'm so sorry."

"It's okay. My middle toes got the worst of it."

"I don't know what happened. I—"

"It's okay," he repeated, smiling at her. "I'll be fine."

Something fluttered in her chest. Confused, Jeri crouched over the fallen block, dug her hands beneath it, lifted it to her body and stood, pushing up with her legs. She *had* carried these heavy salt blocks many times. She knew exactly how to handle them without injuring herself. Or anyone else. And she knew that if she had dropped that heavy block on her own foot, she would be angry and shouting words she ought not to say. Wondering why he hadn't reacted in similar fashion, she carried the heavy block to the truck.

Something didn't add up. She'd done a lot of reading about the side effects of long-term anabolic steroid use, and nothing she had seen so far, other than the sheer size of the man, indicated what she knew—which was that Ryder Smith was an abuser of the drug. What was going on? He shouldn't be able to control his reactions like this.

She turned to find Ryder carrying a second block from the storage room. He walked with a decided limp. She wanted to slink away and hide, but she reminded herself that this big, handsome cowboy had killed her baby brother in a fit of rage. Someone had to figure out what was going on here and reveal the truth.

Unfortunately, she was the only someone who could or would.

Every step hurt, and his two middle toes throbbed incessantly, but Ryder consoled himself with the fact that neither his big toe nor his pinky had been smashed. Either would have made walking far more difficult. He'd soak his foot and tape them, but it would have to wait until they were finished with the southeast section.

Wyatt needed his help before the storm came, and Ryder reasoned that he'd be riding more than walking. Besides, his pride wouldn't let him limp away to lick his wounds. He'd had worse injuries, much worse. It was probably his own fault, anyway. He'd been distracted by standing so close to her while he handed her that block. Maybe he'd fumbled it, making it harder for her to keep her grip.

While Ryder finished loading the mineral blocks, Jeri went to help Wyatt load the sledges and harnesses in the back of the truck. Then she helped him turn the unsaddled horses out into the corral and walk their saddled mounts to the truck. Jeri held Pearl's reins while Ryder and Wyatt tied their respective mounts to the end of the trailer.

"Why aren't we hauling the horses?" she asked.

"Well, we'd normally use Delgado's truck or Jake's," Ryder told her. "But Delgado's off today, and since Jake opened his mechanic's shop, his truck is often in use."

"I have a truck," Jeri pointed out. "My trailer's over at the Burns place, but if you have one, I could—"

"We'll trail 'em," Wyatt decreed. "It's not that far. Thanks anyway."

Trailing the horses meant slow going; not that Ryder would've minded if his foot hadn't ached like a whole mouthful of rotten teeth. Still, he said nothing as Jeri got into the back seat of Wyatt's truck cab. Wyatt took the driver's seat and slowly pulled the rig out of the barn, flatbed and horses behind them. Ryder closed the doors and limped over to crawl into the front passenger seat.

"Are you sure you're okay?" Wyatt asked as Ryder wiggled his toes, trying to ease them.

"I'm fine. I don't think they're broken."

"You ought to know," Wyatt muttered. "You've had more than your fair share of broken toes."

"Comes with the territory," Ryder said, twisting to smile at Jeri, in case she was feeling bad about dropping that block. She winced slightly and turned her gaze out the side window.

Ryder faced forward and reached for the handle of his door as Wyatt brought the truck to a stop in front of the main gate.

"No, no," Wyatt said, throwing the transmission into Park. "I'll get the gate. You stay off that foot while you can."

An awkward silence filled the truck cab as Wyatt left them to push the heavy gate open.

Ryder twisted around in his seat again, worried that

Jeri might be fretting. Or maybe he just wanted to look at her. She'd pulled her hair back into a loose ponytail at the nape of her neck, covering her ears. Those big brown eyes stared at him from beneath the brim of her hat. He'd never seen anything prettier. He felt like he was fifteen again, trying to work up the nerve to speak to the most popular girl in school.

"I hope you won't be too cold out there," he finally said. He just couldn't think of anything else.

"I'll be all right," she told him, pulling a long red muffler from a coat pocket and draping it around her neck. She held up her hands, showing him the leather palms of her matching red knit gloves. "See? All toasty."

He reached behind him and pulled out his own gloves then held up them up to show them off. Made of thick, supple leather with slit cuffs that could be rolled down, they were the best work gloves he'd ever possessed.

"Stark turned us on to this brand. The linings can be removed for washing. Or for summer."

She nodded but said nothing. So much for putting her at ease with conversation. He pulled on his gloves in silence.

Wyatt opened the door and got in. He slowly guided the rig into the pasture, making sure to clear the horses before putting the transmission into Park again.

Ryder opened his door. He wanted away from Jeri Bogman for a few moments to clear his head. He couldn't figure out what to make of her. She looked as sweet as cotton candy, but she had a certain coolness about her that he found puzzling. "I'll close the gate."

At the same time, she said, "Let me get it."

She opened her door and bailed out just as he attempted to pass by. They collided. She bounced off him, reeling backward. He caught her before she could hit the truck, his hands clamping onto her upper arms. She looked up, her eyes huge in her sweet face. Something hot and electric flowed between them. Gasping, she jerked back as if he'd burned her.

"S-Sorry!" She made a face as if to say, "I'm such a klutz." Then she turned toward the gate and trotted away.

Frowning, Ryder got back into the truck.

"That woman is dangerous," Wyatt muttered.

"You're telling me," Ryder said with a chuckle.

She was the most dangerous woman he'd ever come across.

With the gate safely closed behind them, they drove through pasture after pasture, passing big round hay bales. Wyatt stopped the truck and got out to set down mineral blocks, stripping them of their plastic covers and tossing the resulting detritus into the back of the truck for disposal later. They'd put out water troughs at the sites with windmills next to the fenced plots where their late uncle, Dodd, had started growing sod, which had turned out to be a major cash crop for the ranch. As long as the water was pumping, they didn't have to worry too much about ice forming, but it was safer to lock down the windmills in cold weather like this. Ryder used a ball peen hammer to break up the ice on the surface of the troughs so the cattle could drink.

At every stop, Jeri checked the horses and surveyed the surrounding land with curious eyes. She had lots of questions, which Wyatt answered, succinctly at first and then with growing detail as he responded to her enthusiasm. It was obvious that cultivating grass as a cash crop intrigued her.

"Raising cattle is a risky business," Wyatt told her. "You have to hedge your bets any way you can. How Dodd came across this idea, I don't know, but it's a good one if you've got enough land and the right soil compositions."

Ryder noticed that Jeri became much more relaxed and animated when she was talking about ranching, animals or grass. She warmed to each subject as it arose, engaging happily with Wyatt, but she ignored Ryder pointedly. He didn't know whether to be glad or sad about that.

When they got to the ravine that would serve as their staging area, they parked the truck and got out to load the hay and remaining mineral blocks onto the sledges, which they lined up side by side. Ryder worked to secure the load on the middle sledge with rubber tie-downs while surreptitiously watching Jeri struggle to do the same on another sledge to his right. She reached across with her left hand to secure the hook at the end of the tie-down in a small metal loop on the sledge, but the loop popped free, allowing the rubber strip to snap back in Jeri's direction.

Instantly, Ryder lurched to the side, knocking her out of range of the rebounding tie-down and the metal hook attached to its end. She hit the ground with an "Oof!" and Ryder landed right beside her, the heavy rubber strap snapping over his head.

For a moment, nothing and no one moved. It was as if the world simply stopped for the space of a heartbeat. Then suddenly, fear hit Ryder. He knew too well how quickly tragedy could change everything. He scrambled to his knees, shaking off his gloves, and laid hands on Jeri to make sure the metal hook hadn't somehow caught her. As stunned as he, she stared at him while he checked her head and shoulders for injuries. He found no lump or gash, but before he could explore further, she rolled away.

Suddenly, Wyatt was there, reaching down a hand to each of them, his face set like stone, lips taut as he hauled them up.

"Anyone hurt?"

They both shook their heads while dusting themselves off.

Wyatt closed his eyes and sucked in a deep, calming breath. For a moment, Ryder feared that his big brother was about to blow his stack. Of all the Smith brothers, Wyatt had the hottest temper, though he kept it under control. He could, in fact, be exceedingly patient. Tina's pregnancy, the coming storm and the biting cold had combined to fray his nerves, however, and Ryder wouldn't have been surprised if any little thing pushed Wyatt over the edge.

"Are you two trying to maim each other?" Wyatt growled.

Jeri shook dust from her hair and bent to snatch up her hat.

"The anchor came loose," Ryder said quickly, picking up his own hat and gloves. He paused to watch her slap cold, red dust from her clothing. "You sure you're okay?"

She nodded and sent him a wry smile. "Guess it's my day for accidents."

He chuckled and reached out to sweep away a blot of dust that she'd missed on her sleeve. Her eyes widened. The next instant, her face hardened, as if a mask had slipped into place, and she jerked back. Ryder dropped his hand as Wyatt started beating the dust off him. Embarrassed, Ryder brushed off his brother's hands. He wasn't five years old anymore, and Wyatt had no reason to treat him as if he was. Besides, a little dirt never hurt anybody.

Muttering, "I'll get the harnesses," Ryder trudged over to the truck bed while Wyatt helped Jeri secure her load.

With the load safely tied down with rope, Wyatt took a harness from Ryder and went back to his own sledge and horse. Ryder helped Jeri hitch up her horse.

"This is an ingenious rig," Jeri commented, stepping up beside him as he went to work on his big red dun, Handy. "Simple. Efficient. Best of all, I see no way this could harm the horse."

"It's a good system," Ryder agreed. "Our uncle invented it. There was talk of a patent, but we're not sure he ever did anything about that."

"Maybe you should," she said. "I think you could manufacture and sell this."

"Worth considering," he commented, grinning.

Abruptly, as if she'd just remembered something important, she strode to the Perlino's head, abandoning Ryder and the conversation.

Ryder lifted his eyebrows. What a strange female. Strange and lovely.

He tightened the girth on the dun's saddle before securing the load on his sledge. While he hooked the tie-down into place, Jeri efficiently tightened the girth on Pearl's saddle. Wyatt swung up onto his big gray, Blue Moon. Pearl's reins in hand, Jeri shifted around to the side, as if preparing to mount. She paused to watch Ryder stand and give his load a final check.

"Watch it!" Wyatt warned.

Ryder looked up in time to see Pearl, who was something of a clown, curl her neck and throw her head, butting Jeri right between the shoulder blades. Ryder straightened as Jeri launched toward him, the reins falling to the ground. Pearl placidly faced forward again, the equine equivalent of feigned innocence. Ryder, meanwhile, found himself clutching an astonished female with curves not even a down coat could disguise. Mouth agape, eyes wide, she stared up at him from beneath the brim of her hat. He tightened his arms and smiled to let her know she was safe. She hadn't, after all, hit the cold, hard ground this time. He realized that he was staring at her lips when her gaze dropped to his.

Ryder didn't know what might have happened if Wyatt hadn't burst out laughing. At the sound, Jeri jerked away, flouncing off to gather Pearl's reins. She trod on Ryder's foot in the process, the uninjured one, thankfully. He grimaced but kept his groan inside.

Jeri climbed onto Pearl. Shaking his head, Wyatt led off. Ryder gestured for Jeri to follow then limped around to mount. As he and Handy fell in behind her, Ryder knew exactly what his big brother was thinking. But *dangerous* didn't scratch the surface of the peril that Jeri Bogman brought with her.

The woman was positively lethal.

In more ways that Ryder dared contemplate.

Chapter Three

Guilt and regret washed over Jeri as Wyatt stalked back to shut the gate behind the truck, trailer and horses, muttering that they were returning to the house over two hours later than they should've been. Their tardiness was, of course, her fault. After her unexpected reaction when she'd found herself in Ryder's arms, she'd purposefully made every "mistake" she could while "helping" the Smith brothers provide for their cattle. She'd been hoping for an angry outburst from Ryder to remind her why she was right to hate him—and why it was wrong to find his arms around her so very appealing.

It wouldn't have been an easy morning even without her interference. That being the case, something should have set off Ryder's temper. Obviously, he was on his best behavior in front of company. Still, she reasoned that she was at least nettling him, priming the pump, so to speak. Eventually, given enough provocation, he'd surely lose control. Wouldn't he?

Unfortunately, the only one she'd managed to upset thus far was Wyatt, and she couldn't be happy about adding to the weight on his shoulders. He was a man with a lot on his mind.

Wyatt had called his wife to be sure she was okay and let her know they would be late for lunch. Jeri noticed that Ryder had calmly, gently tried to reassure his brother. Though he addressed himself to Jeri now, his words were clearly aimed at Wyatt as the older brother climbed back into the truck.

"Takes a lot of strength to carry twins, but that's Tina for you. No challenge too big for her. Why, you should've seen the state the house was in when she first came. And, of course, she'll do anything for the sake of her husband and kids, even put up with his lazy brothers."

"And which brothers would those be?" Wyatt asked, putting the transmission into gear and starting the rig forward again. "You and Jake have worked your fingers to the bone getting the place in shape."

"That reminds me," Ryder said. "Now that the B and B and the shop are fully operational, I'm going to help Jake do some work around his and Kathryn's place after the weather warms up. They want to add an office and a third bedroom."

"Sounds good."

Wyatt pulled the truck up to the small door on the stable end of the barn. Ryder got out and went to untie the horses. Jeri went to help him. She didn't intend to apologize, but she couldn't seem to help herself.

"I'm sorry if I made us late."

"Aw, no," Ryder said, tossing her that shy, boyish smile so at odds with his muscular build, heavy beard shadow and deep voice. "We'd have taken even longer without your help."

"I'm not sure Wyatt would agree."

"Wyatt knows you didn't intentionally slow us down."

Except she had, and that knowledge shamed Jeri even as she rationalized it in her mind.

They got the horses to their stalls. Jeri volunteered to open the big, central barn doors while Ryder began unsaddling. She left Wyatt backing the truck and trailer into the barn and went to help Ryder brush down and feed the horses. After unhooking the trailer, Wyatt came to help bring in the other mounts and lend a hand with stowing the tack.

As they worked, the two men discussed the proposed renovations to their brother's house. Jeri listened with fascination and no little envy as they mulled ways to get Jake to accept their assistance, monetary and otherwise. These brothers obviously cared for one another and supported each other wholeheartedly.

The temperature had risen several degrees while they were out, leading everyone to unbutton their coats and peel off their mufflers as they'd worked. Now, with all the horses again inside the draped stable area, the place soon felt toasty warm. Ryder removed his coat and hung it on a recessed hook. Jeri did the same, but Wyatt kept his on.

"Hurry it up," he ordered as he went to pull the truck out of the barn and close the big doors. "Otherwise you'll be eating dinner instead of lunch."

"Be right behind you," Ryder called. He shook his head, chuckling.

"Did I miss something?" Jeri asked. She hadn't heard anything funny in Wyatt's tone or words.

"I was just thinking that Wyatt can't stand being away

from Tina for any length of time. It was that way even before he started worrying about her and the babies."

"What's to worry about?" she asked. "Women have been having babies since the Garden of Eden. Is there cause for concern?"

Ryder shrugged and dropped the curry brushes into the work bucket. "She's been having some cramps, I think. Doctor says to just keep an eye on it."

Jeri couldn't help wanting to put him at ease. "Way I hear it, that's pretty common in the last months of pregnancy—it's the body's way of getting ready to deliver."

Ryder looked at her, his brow creased with concern. "The babies aren't due until April."

In other words, the first week of January was much too soon to deliver a healthy baby, let alone twins. Jeri nodded, now sharing his concern.

"I'll pray for them."

The smile he sent her was so sweet that she had to shut her eyes against it. He picked up his jacket and the bucket. She grabbed her own coat and followed him as he carried the curry bucket into the tack room. He came out a heartbeat later, shrugging into his jacket, but when she swung hers around to do likewise, he caught it by the shoulders and helped her into it.

Why that felt like such an intimate gesture, Jeri didn't know. It wasn't as if she'd never before been helped into her coat by a handsome cowboy. She told herself it was just because she was predisposed to dislike him but somehow couldn't. Not yet. Not until he showed his true colors. Once the man who had killed her brother came out, it would be different. Wouldn't it?

They walked across the dusty yard in silence. As soon as they stepped up into the carport, Ryder peeled off his gloves and stuffed them into his coat pockets. They reached the back door. Ryder opened it and stood aside to let her enter first.

Warmth hit her in a wave, letting her know just how cold it really was out there. As she shucked her gloves and coat, hanging the latter on the back of a chair at the table, she saw that Wyatt hadn't waited for them before starting to eat. Tina fluttered around, dishing seconds onto his plate from an enormous potpie in the center of the table and then calling Jeri and Ryder over to eat. They obeyed, washing their hands side by side at the kitchen sink before picking up plates from the counter. Ryder dished food onto Jeri's plate before helping himself. Jeri set her plate in front of the chair with her coat.

Another man occupied a chair at the table. Even if he hadn't been holding Kathryn Smith's hand, Jeri would have known he was the middle Smith brother. Jake was as tall as his brothers and had the same dark eyes and heavy beard shadow, but his hair was more brown like Wyatt's than black like Ryder's, and he wasn't as heavily built as the other two. Ryder set his plate on the table and introduced them.

"Jeri, this here is our brother Jacoby. Jake, Jeri Bogman."

Jake nodded at Jeri but spoke to Ryder. "Heard you've had quite a day already."

"Nothing much out of the ordinary," Ryder said lightly, pulling out the chair for Jeri.

She glanced around, feeling surprised by that small gesture and foolish for the surge of pleasure it had given her. Ryder stood with his hand on his own chair while she took her seat, aware that everyone was looking at her. Only after she was seated did Ryder pull out the chair next to her and drop down into it.

"How come you're so late then?" Jake asked. "I thought I was gonna have to go looking for y'all."

Ryder calmly started eating. "No need for that. So, how's business? This storm going to put a kink in things?"

"Already has." Jake talked about charging batteries at two different farms that morning. "The cold weather zaps a weak battery. But I wound up hauling in a broken-down Jeep for restoration. Thing must be sixty years old."

"Which means you can't wait to get your hands on it," Ryder said, grinning.

"Mechanics make house calls here?" Jeri asked.

Everyone else laughed. "Mechanics, veterinarians, doctors, even the grocer if the need is great enough," Ryder said.

"The grocer in town kindly delivered for us a few times after Mom first came home from the hospital," Kathryn said softly, "but he's so limited in what he can offer." A brief explanation of the accident that had paralyzed Kathryn's mother followed.

"Folks have to be real neighborly when most conveniences are thirty or forty miles away," Ryder commented.

"I don't mind driving out to help someone," Jake said, glancing at Jeri. "Good way to scope out the surrounding area."

Obviously, he'd been told that she was shopping for property.

"If this storm is as bad as they're predicting," she said, "I may have to wait a few days to start looking around."

Jake rose then. "Speaking of the weather, I better get back to the shop while I can." Grinning at Ryder, he added, "Unless the roads ice over, I've only got an hour or so to tear into that Jeep before Dean drops off his grandmother's car for new brakes." Kathryn quickly rose and followed her husband to the door, where the two whispered farewells and briefly kissed.

Leaning toward Jeri, Ryder softly muttered, "Newlyweds."

The sound, so close to Jeri's ear, sent shivers through her. Frowning, she leaned forward and focused on her plate. That wasn't the thrill of attraction, she told herself; that was revulsion. Whatever it was, it sank her mood into the doldrums.

Wyatt quickly finished his meal and got up to carry his plate to the sink. Kathryn rinsed it and placed it in the dishwasher while Wyatt headed toward the door.

"Where are you off to now?" Tina asked, following him.

"I'm going to rearrange the storage room," he told her. "Since Jake moved out, it's been a jumble in there."

"He says he left some things behind," Kathryn remarked. "If you'll set aside anything of his, we'll get it out of your way."

"Sounds like a plan," Wyatt told her, taking his coat from a peg on the wall.

Ryder gulped down a big bite and pushed back his chair. "I'll help you."

"No, no. You've barely had time to warm up. Finish eating, then go lift your precious weights or see if Jake needs help. Better yet, see to that foot."

As Wyatt pulled his gloves and muffler from his coat, what sounded like a herd of cattle rumbled down the stairs. A heartbeat later, two small boys and two dogs ran into the room. The dogs, one a pup, went straight to the food and water bowls next to the stove and parked there hopefully, tails wagging.

The older boy, a strawberry blond whose shirtsleeves were too short, went to Tina, declaring, "We're hungry, Mom. Can we have a snack?"

"You just had lunch."

"Actually, that was nearly three hours ago," Kathryn said, catching the smaller boy, who threw his arms around her.

Tina sighed. "Oh, all right. Dinner will be late, anyway."

The dogs gave up their vigil at the food bowls and moved to the door as Wyatt, who had finished outfitting himself for the cold, reached for the knob.

"Let the dogs go with you, dear," Tina said, "and don't stay out there too long."

"Don't worry about me," he told her. "Love you."

"Love you, too."

He allowed the dogs to follow him through the door, pulling it closed behind them.

"KKay, I want stauburries," the smaller boy announced.

Kathryn smoothed her hand over his dark head. "We don't have any *strawberries*." She pronounced the word carefully. "How about sliced apples and peanut butter for a snack?"

"Yay!"

He ran to Ryder, who drew the boy up to straddle his knee. "Unca Ryder, we got apples an' peanut budder. Want some?"

"No, thanks." Ryder hugged the boy. "I'm having

another helping of this potpie, though." Ryder reached around the child to serve himself.

"What's this about your foot?" Tina asked, waddling back to the table.

Before he could answer, the boy on Ryder's knee pointed a finger at Jeri. "Who dat?"

"That's Miss Jeri," Ryder answered. "She's our guest." He waved a hand between the two boys, saying to Jeri, "These are my nephews, Tyler and Frankie."

Jeri made herself smile at the boys, but she felt off-balance. Ryder Smith wasn't supposed to be a helpful brother and doting uncle. He wasn't supposed to make her shiver or want to join in the conversation. He shouldn't be long-suffering and patient. She shouldn't appreciate his handling of the horses or find him the most attractive of the Smith brothers. He was a fiend, a villain.

Kathryn brought over two small plates filled with sliced apples, crackers and globs of peanut butter. Frankie slid off Ryder's knee and right onto his foot. Ryder grimaced.

"Ryder Dodd Smith," Tina said, folding her arms above the swell of her belly. "What did you do to your foot?"

He shrugged sheepishly. "Something fell on it."

Jeri tried not to wince as guilt swept through her. She told herself that he deserved a couple of smashed toes, but she couldn't quite believe it somehow. Especially when he protected her by leaving her culpability out of it.

Tina rolled her eyes. "Get that boot off." She turned toward the back of the house, saying, "Kathryn, we're going to need some hot water and then ice packs. I'll get the Epsom salts."

Sighing, Ryder sent an apologetic glance at Jeri and started eating again. Kathryn went to heat water.

Feeling as slimy as a slug, Jeri beat a hasty retreat, mumbling that she needed to make a phone call. If she didn't speak to her mother soon, she was going to lose her nerve. These Smiths were too…normal…too likable, especially Ryder.

As she climbed the stairs, she heard something hitting the roof of the house. Too sharp to be rain and too light to be hail, the sound grew louder as she reached the landing and made her way down the hall to her room. Pushing aside the ruffled curtain, she looked out at the crystalline ice beginning to coat the bare limbs of the trees in the side yard. Within moments, the lawn was sparkling white and the outside of the window had begun to glaze over.

Jeri felt trapped in a prison of her own making.

No. She shook her head. Ryder Smith had made this prison for her family when he killed her little brother. And he had to pay for that. God was going to make him pay for that. She had to believe God would make him pay.

For her own sake, as well as her mother's, she must make sure of it.

Pulling her small phone from the pocket of her jeans, she found her mom's phone number and made the call.

"It's getting nasty out there," Kathryn remarked, closing the door behind the dogs, both of which shook themselves off before plopping down on the rug in front of the cookstove.

"Hope this doesn't last too long," Ryder commented, pulling on his sock.

Soaking his foot had made his toes throb like a big brass drum, but the ice packs had helped calm the throb. And the over-the-counter analgesic Tina had given him, coupled with the way Kathryn had taped two of the toes together, was taking the edge off what remained.

"Kathryn," Tina said, "maybe you, Jake and Frankie should spend the night here."

Kathryn nodded. As Ryder gingerly pushed his injured foot down into his boot, Tina made a sound that pretty well described how it felt to shove broken toes into a cowboy boot. When he looked over at her, though, he saw that she was grasping her belly, her face screwed up in pain.

"Tina!" Kathryn yelped, rushing to her side.

At the same time, Tyler cried, "Mom!"

Gasping harshly, Tina reached out and steadied herself by grabbing Kathryn's shoulder. She seemed to catch her breath and straightened, only to cry out and double over again. Making a gargling sound, she started to sink. Ryder jumped up and caught her, sweeping her into his arms as she groaned.

"Call the doctor!" he barked, carrying Tina toward the bedroom she shared with Wyatt. Thankfully, the bedroom was on the ground floor and just down the hall from the kitchen. Behind him, Tyler and Frankie slid off their chairs. "Stay where you are, boys!" he ordered.

"The n-number's on my phone," Tina managed, clutching his neck with one arm and digging for her phone with the other hand.

Kathryn caught up with them and took the phone as Ryder lowered Tina onto the big bed. Tina curled onto her side, gasping again. Before Ryder could straighten, she grabbed him by the shirtsleeve.

"Get Wyatt."

"Right away."

He hurried for the door while Kathryn made the phone call. Tina moaned again; it was a strangled, frightened sound. Looking back in concern, Ryder strode into the hall—and straight into Jeri Bogman.

"Oh!"

He quickly stepped around her, his hands steadying her by the shoulders. "I've got to find Wyatt."

"Something wrong?"

He glanced back into the bedroom before quickly ushering her away from the door, toward the kitchen. "Tina could be in labor," he said in a low, tense voice.

"Oh, no. Can I do anything?"

"Keep an eye on the boys," he said, leaving her at the kitchen table as he rushed for his coat. As he yanked open the door, he heard Jeri urging the boys to return to the table. Ryder hurried outside, throwing on his coat and praying silently as he went.

Thankfully, the new carport covered the steps, so they were dry and clear. The ground, however, was already slick with ice, which continued to fall in angry, wet splatters. Nevertheless, he ran, his injured foot screaming with every step. Slipping and flailing his arms to maintain balance, he got to the barn and went in through the small door, calling for his brother.

"Wyatt! Wyatt!" He heard the distant bang of a plank door.

"Ryder?"

He got as far as the middle section of the barn before Wyatt appeared out of the gloom.

"What's wrong?"

"Tina's in pain. Kathryn's calling the doctor."

Wyatt took off at a dead run.

"Watch the ice!" Ryder yelled, going after him.

Ryder caught up with Wyatt as he grabbed the edge of the barn's door to keep his feet from going out from under him. He mentally reminded himself to come out later, when the onslaught had stopped, and sprinkle rock salt on the ground around the house and barn. For now, Ryder focused on following Wyatt across the yard as quickly as he could possibly manage in the horrible conditions. He didn't want to think about trying to drive Tina to the hospital in Ardmore. As he followed his brother to the house, he resumed his fervent prayers.

Please, God. Please don't let them lose their babies. I've given Wyatt enough heartache already. Please don't let them lose their babies.

The next hour passed at a crawl, with Wyatt and Tina closed in the bedroom and Kathryn going in and out. The boys caught the gloomy atmosphere. Their snacks abandoned, they looked around with wide, worried eyes. Finally, Jeri interceded.

"Say, why don't you guys show me your room? Bet we can find something to do there."

"My room," Tyler clarified.

"I got a room!" Frankie insisted. "I got two." He held up two fingers in case Jeri didn't understand, adding, "With puppies."

"You just nap in the room here," Tyler argued. "You live in your room in town."

Jeri lifted her eyebrows at Ryder as she urged the boys toward the stairs. "Let's go upstairs anyway."

Ryder thought that she was good with kids, but the

greater part of his mind was centered on Tina and Wyatt. Minutes crept by. At last Ryder heard a vehicle pull into the carport. Rushing to the door, he recognized the truck and the couple getting out of it. Wes Billings was a local rancher, and his wife, Alice Shorter Billings, was the local doctor. Ryder closed his eyes and whispered a prayer of gratitude as the pair hurried toward the steps.

"I'm so glad you're here," Ryder told them.

"Tina's OB called me," Alice said. "I came as soon as I could."

"Thank you so much."

He stepped back to let them enter then led the way to the bedroom. After tapping on the door, he opened it.

"Wes and Dr. Alice are here."

Wyatt rose from the chair beside the bed and came to greet them. Wes carried her medical bag into the room, smiled at Wyatt and Tina, left the bag on the chair Wyatt had just vacated, and backed out again, pulling the door closed behind him. Suddenly, Jeri was at Ryder's elbow.

"We heard a vehicle arrive. Frankie says it's the doctor."

"My wife," Wes supplied. "She's in with Tina now."

Ryder quickly made introductions. "Uh, our guest, Jeri Bogman. And Wes Billings."

Wes shook Jeri's hand then lifted an eyebrow at Ryder.

"I'm the official house-call barista," he said. "How about a cup of coffee?"

"It's already made," Ryder muttered, fighting the impulse to stand by the bedroom door and listen in case he was needed.

Wes's next words pulled him away.

"Coffee and prayer," Wes said. "Being married to a doctor, I've learned to specialize in both."

"That sounds good to me," Jeri said, lifting a hand to Ryder's shoulder.

That small hand comforted him in a way he couldn't describe. Coffee and prayer with Jeri beside him sounded good.

In fact, they sounded essential.

He turned, giving her the best smile he could muster, and led the way back into the kitchen.

Chapter Four

Sitting silently beside Jeri at the kitchen table as Wes voiced a prayer, Ryder found himself thinking about reaching for Jeri's hand. He told himself that the impulse came from his family's habit of holding hands while giving thanks for the food at mealtimes, but the truth was that focusing fully on the prayer required a good deal of effort. Jake's arrival was a welcome distraction. Kathryn, who had just refilled coffee cups, abandoned the carafe on the kitchen counter and went to greet him.

"Have any trouble getting here?"

He shook his head, hanging his coat on a wall peg. "It's just a couple hundred yards. Besides, I put snow chains on the truck."

Dr. Alice came into the room. Placing her medical kit on the end of the kitchen table, she plopped down in the chair next to her husband and let out a long sigh. Across from her, Ryder noticed a sprinkling of silver in her sleek blond hair, which she wore in a neat chignon at the nape of her neck. Somehow, though, both she and Wes looked younger than they had before they'd married only months earlier. Watching Wes pat her hand, Ryder felt a stab of envy. He couldn't help feeling that everyone around him was paired up except him. He struggled to turn off the thought, reminding himself that he had too many strikes against him to hope for romance.

Mentally, he ticked off the reasons he shouldn't expect to find himself part of a couple. He had no real occupation, lived mainly on the largesse of his brothers, and he'd killed a man. What woman would find that attractive? None. Obviously.

Jake's voice broke into his thoughts. "How is Tina?"

The doctor answered. "Well, the medication has stopped her contractions for now. She's resting comfortably."

"It was Braxton-Hicks, then?" Kathryn asked hopefully. "I've heard it's quite common."

Dr. Alice shook her head. "In my experience, Braxton-Hicks contractions are much milder than what Tina described—and they come later in the pregnancy. But then, with twins, who can say? I've ordered her to stay in bed until she can see her ob-gyn."

Kathryn looked to Jake, who immediately responded.

"I could drive her and Wyatt over to Ardmore. I've not had much experience with snow chains, but if we take it slow…"

Dr. Alice nodded. "If her contractions start up again, she'll need to get straight to the emergency room at the hospital in Ardmore. Otherwise, she'll be fine until she sees her ob-gyn on Thursday."

"We'll stay over tonight," Kathryn said. "Just in case." She smiled at Jake. "I've already made up the beds."

Holding his wife's gaze, Jake nodded. "Sure thing, honey."

Ryder marveled that even after nearly three months of marriage, Kathryn could still blush when Jake called her "honey" in front of others.

"I—I'd better start dinner," she said, sounding a little breathless.

"I'll help you," Ryder volunteered.

"Me, too," Jeri added.

Nodding, Kathryn addressed Wes and Alice. "Won't you stay and join us?"

Wes shook his head and pushed back his chair. "Best not. If we get any more precipitation, we'd be here for the duration." He grinned at Jake. "We native Oklahomans don't travel on snow chains. Never even thought of it."

Jake chuckled. "Being from Houston, I ordered a few sets just to be on the safe side."

"That was probably a good impulse," Wes mused, "even if you don't use them more than a day or two a year."

"I have them," Jeri said. "There are some big rodeos in really snowy places, but they're a pain to hook up on my own, so I don't use them much."

"Interesting," Wes said. He looked to Alice. "Given how often she gets called out, I might ought to invest in a set."

"I'll remind you of that the next time we get called out in the ice," Alice said dryly, "and there's not a set on the place."

Wes chuckled. "How well she knows me. We'd better scoot, Dr. Wife."

Alice smiled as she rose. "Call if you need me," she

said to the room at large as she made her way around the table.

Wes retrieved the medical bag from the end of the table just as Wyatt came into the kitchen. "You folks leaving?"

"We are," Wes confirmed.

Hurrying to them, Wyatt hugged Alice and clapped Wes on the back. "Thank you so much for coming out in this."

"That's the life of a small-town doctor," Wes told him. "And her husband." He slid an arm across Alice's shoulders, and they moved toward the door together.

While Wyatt saw them into their coats and out the door, the boys came downstairs and went straight to Kathryn.

"Aunt KKay, we're hungry again," Tyler whined.

"I'm starting dinner now," she told them, "but you can have some graham crackers, if you like. Just a few."

Tyler ran to the pantry, but Frankie went to Jake and crawled up in his lap. "Aunt Tina sleepin'," he reported in a small voice.

Ryder caught the note of concern, and he wasn't the only one.

"That's good," Jeri told the boy, "for her and her babies. When I was little, my mother spent months in bed. I thought she was just napping all the time, but she was growing a baby brother for me."

"Aunt Tina growing *two* babies. She gotta sleep a bunch," Frankie reasoned, sounding much more confident about the situation.

Ryder chuckled. Jake and Kathryn frequently corrected Frankie's speech, but Ryder loved the way the boy expressed himself.

"Do you have a lot of siblings?" Jake asked Jeri.

Ryder noticed that she stiffened, her gaze downcast. "No. I think Mom would've liked more, but it wasn't possible."

"Ah."

Jeri got up from the table then and turned to Kathryn. "How can I help?"

Kathryn looked at Wyatt as he walked toward the table. "Would Tina like anything in particular?"

"She said something about soup."

"Beef and barley or chicken noodle?"

"Beef and barley," all three brothers said at once.

One of the best things about a true winter, Ryder had decided, was Kathryn's beef and barley soup.

Kathryn shrugged at Jeri. "Can you chop vegetables?"

"Sure."

"I'll do the onion and celery if you'll take care of the carrots and green beans."

"I'll get the beef, zucchini and wheat rolls out of the freezer," Ryder said, moving in that direction as Tyler carried the graham cracker box to Jake, who began doling out the crackers one quarter at a time.

When the boys had eaten as much as Jake would allow, he took them into the den to watch television. Wyatt looked in on Tina then walked out with Ryder to spread rock salt and check the horses. Thankfully, the sleet had stopped.

"I hope no one's wounded before dinner gets on the table," Wyatt drawled. "That Jeri is a walking catastrophe."

"Aw, she's not that bad," Ryder replied casually.

"What I can't figure," Wyatt went on, "is how such a clumsy girl could make it to the national finals."

Ryder chuckled. "If you didn't notice, she's a natural on horseback."

"That's true," Wyatt conceded. "Let's hope she's as skilled with a paring knife."

Nodding, Ryder silently noted that as it was his foot that was throbbing, he ought to be the one irritated with her rather than Wyatt, but for some reason he couldn't quite manage it. Despite her hot and cold nature, something about her felt…right. He had to think she meant well, and she'd been sweet and helpful with the boys and Kathryn.

"Suppose I better use Jake's truck to take Jeri over to Stark's later." He slid a glance at Wyatt from the corner of his eye. "She helped us earlier. Turnabout's only fair. Besides, I'd like to get a look at those animals of hers."

"No doubt you would. You've had horses on the brain for a while now."

Deciding this was not the time to press for a horse-raising operation at the ranch, Ryder said nothing.

After a particularly satisfying dinner—during the preparation of which no one, thankfully, suffered any injury—Jake and Wyatt got the boys ready for bed while Ryder and Jeri helped Kathryn clean up the kitchen. Tina had eaten a hearty meal, and Kathryn announced her intention to sit with her for a while, so Ryder proposed taking Jeri over to Stark's in Jake's truck to care for her horses. Surprisingly, she hesitated before agreeing.

"Yes, I guess that would be best."

Ryder fetched Jake's keys, and he and Jeri outfitted themselves for the cold. One thing Ryder disliked about a true winter was having to constantly dress and undress to deal with the weather, but he couldn't manage the cold without a coat or sit around a toasty house in one. A stiff breeze had blown up, and he couldn't keep from commenting on it once he and Jeri were inside Jake's truck.

"Man, that wind cuts right through you, don't it?"

"It does," she agreed, shivering. "But it's a good thing. Not only will it blow away the clouds, it will help dry up and blow away the ice."

She was right about that. The sky had already cleared, and stars were beginning to twinkle as the pickup trundled toward the Burns compound. Ryder had no experience with snow chains, but they didn't have far to travel, and the truck moved along the icy roadway with ungainly ease. Even traveling slowly, they turned off the highway onto the Burns compound in less than ten minutes.

After guiding the truck past the veterinary clinic and around the neatly constructed stables, Ryder came to a halt with the headlights shining on the padlocked door. Jeri had a key and used it to let herself into the building. Ryder shut off the engine and followed her inside.

Unlike the old-fashioned barn at Loco Man, this low, metal building had every modern convenience, including excellent lighting. Ryder moved through a set of heavy plastic drapes and past the first stall, which held a horse bearing a large incision on its neck. He could see stitches beneath a length of what looked like clear tape. Several empty stalls stood between the wounded horse and a second set of drapes. Beyond that, he found Jeri's beauties.

The four bays—three mares and one stud—were so

similar that they looked like a matched set. They had
the glossiest hides and firmest conformation Ryder had
ever seen. All of a height, they would produce equally
beautiful offspring. He let out a long, low whistle.

"Where on earth did you come by these lovelies?"

Jeri shrugged, rubbing the neck of one horse while
reaching out a hand to another in the next stall. "Here
and there. Glad's Texas born and bred. That's short for
Gladiator. The girls are Star, Betty and Dovie. I picked
up Star in Georgia. Her registered name is Harper's Star-
light. Betty, or Better Betty, came from Wyoming, and I
found Dovie, also known as Stellar Dove, in Colorado."

Dovie was obviously pregnant.

"Well, you've got a good eye," Ryder praised. "If
you're as good at training as you are at choosing horse-
flesh, you're going to be very successful."

Jeri smiled. It felt like the first unguarded, truly sincere smile she'd given him. Encouraged, Ryder searched
for something else to say. He didn't know enough about
barrel racing to even ask intelligent questions, so he
talked about his own ambitions, instead, hoping it would
establish a point of common interest between them.

"I'd like to raise horses. Don't know a thing about
training them except to the saddle. Uncle Dodd made
sure all us boys could work an unbroken horse around
to letting us ride, but that's not the same as training for
a specific purpose, like barrel racing."

"It's not too far off," she said. "You might think about
learning how to train cutting horses. They're valued on
a ranch, and there's lots of competition. You can earn
some big money at that."

"I'll have to look into it. You ever trained a cutting
horse?"

"No, no. I don't know much more about it than you do, but you can go online and research it."

He nodded. "Good advice. Thanks."

"Uh-huh."

That seemed to exhaust that topic, at least for now, but then it occurred to him that they had something in common besides a fascination with horses. Specifically, families.

"Does your brother work with horses, too?"

Her smile turned into a frown, and the temperature seemed to drop ten degrees. "No." With that, she sent him a scathing glance, turned her back and stomped toward three sealed barrels.

Stung, Ryder stayed where he was, wondering what he'd said or done to put those angry glints in her eyes. He half expected lightning to shoot out of the top of her head or steam to pour out of her ears. After a moment, he forced himself to ask, "Anything I can do to help?"

She didn't so much as glance in his direction, let alone reply, as she filled a huge scoop with feed and carried it to the first of the horses.

Okay, then. Might as well face facts. Either the girl didn't want him touching her horses or she just didn't much like him. He tried not to be disappointed by either. She had a right to decide who did and didn't care for her horses, just as she had a right not to like him personally. Besides, it wasn't as if anything could come of their acquaintance beyond simple friendship. Why that idea depressed him, he didn't even want to analyze.

Deciding he could at least muck the stalls, Ryder went looking for a shovel and wheelbarrow. Whatever her personal feelings, she surely couldn't object to that. Besides, she'd helped hay the southeast section of the ranch and tend Loco Man's horses. He needed to do something to repay that, and he didn't figure she'd object to him hauling away dung. He worked quietly and carefully, starting with Stark's patient in the other section of the stable, for good measure. As he worked, Jeri went about her own business, making no comment either to commend or criticize. Apparently, she thought him well suited to his chosen chore.

He would remember that in the future.

Ryder Smith was a hard worker; Jeri had to give him that much. Then again, if he was using steroids, he'd need an outlet for the extra energy and agitation that the drugs produced. Twice already, to her shame, she'd forgotten what Ryder had done to her brother, but she remembered now—and was deliberately pushing him to show that side of himself. She expected an explosion soon now.

She both welcomed and dreaded Ryder's temper. On one hand, she needed this matter resolved at last. She needed Ryder held accountable for what he'd done. On the other hand, once Ryder was charged with Bryan's death—or some other punishable activity—he and the Smith family would undoubtedly hate her, and Jeri was unexpectedly saddened by that prospect.

She hadn't expected to like any of these people, but she just couldn't help it. They were a caring, supportive family, and apparently sincere Christians. If her own family had been that supportive and caring, Bryan might not have taken off for Houston at the first opportunity and gotten involved in the sport that would ultimately take his life. And she might not dread visiting or speaking with her own mother.

For too long, since the death of her second husband, Dena Averrett had viewed herself as one of life's greatest victims, and her son's death had only exacerbated that feeling. Angry at the losses she'd suffered, Dena seemed to need to punish someone, and if it wasn't Ryder Smith, it would be her surviving child. Jeri desperately hoped to give her mother some peace, her brother some justice, and herself some relief, even if it wasn't turning out to be as easy as it should've been.

Surprisingly, to this point Ryder had remained downright friendly, no matter what provocation had been thrown at him. Only now did he withdraw. Almost as if she'd hurt his feelings.

Jeri fought the very idea that she might have wounded Ryder emotionally, but it nagged her, wouldn't let her go. Eventually she concluded that being unfriendly would win her nothing. She didn't want him to keep his distance, after all. How could she provoke his temper and prove him volatile enough to have caused her brother's death if he avoided her? If she presented a friendly facade, he might let down his guard. He might even eventually confess his guilt to her or say enough, at least, to prove negligence. Anything was better than nothing, after all.

Regardless, she'd be walking a tightrope. She didn't see any reason to try that balancing act while bearing the additional burden of guilt for having hurt his feelings. It was bad enough that she'd injured his toes. The irony of that did not escape her, but neither did it change anything.

After the horses were settled in for the night and they were walking back to the truck, she tried to bridge the breach by thanking him for his help. "I appreciate you cleaning the stalls. I usually handle all that myself."

He nodded, smiling tautly, and opened the truck door for her. "Only fair. You helped me earlier."

She climbed in and buckled up while he limped around to slide in behind the steering wheel. She said nothing more, and neither did he until they were back in the kitchen of the Loco Man ranch house and he had returned Jake's keys to him. Without sitting or removing his coat, he spent a few minutes regaling his brothers with descriptions of her horses.

"They're gorgeous," he summed up warmly, "all four of them. Once that first crop of foals turns out, I'll be going around saying I once mucked out their stalls."

Jake chuckled. "Only you could get that excited about horses."

"I like horses."

"Lots of people like horses," Jeri blurted, realizing only belatedly that she sounded as if she was defending Ryder.

"Me included," Jake said, "but I wouldn't go out in the cold on a night like this to get a look at any horse."

"You know it was more than that," Wyatt commented to Jake. "He was worried about Jeri driving around without chains. We all were. If he hadn't wanted to see those horses, you or I would've had to take her over there."

Jeri hoped no one noticed her involuntary flinch. These Smith men were unusually thoughtful and protective, not at all the egotistical, arrogant types she'd expected.

"True," Jake said, adding to Jeri. "And I wouldn't have minded a bit."

"You also wouldn't have mucked out the stalls," Wyatt teased.

"And deprive my baby brother of an activity he so obviously enjoys?" Jake quipped.

Ryder rolled his eyes, but his brothers just laughed. Then Wyatt turned serious.

"Maybe we should let him ranch horses like he wants. I'm just not sure there's enough market around here for saddle horses."

"Maybe I should look into getting some training myself," Ryder suggested in a low voice.

"Couldn't hurt," Jake said with a grin. "What are you thinking? Advanced stall mucking?"

"Hey, at least I have some skill," Ryder retorted, laughing at himself.

"You've got plenty of skills," Jake admitted, still grinning. "That's why I'm counting on you to help me build on to our house this spring."

"Done." Ryder changed the subject then. "How's Tina?"

"Sleeping," Wyatt said.

Jake sighed. "That sounds good to me."

"Think I'll hit the hay myself." Ryder turned from the table. "Good night, y'all."

As he limped toward the door, Wyatt said, "We should've had Alice look at your foot while she was here."

Jeri tried to control her wince. "Is it still hurting you?"

Ryder waved a hand. "No, no. It's fine. Just a couple of sore toes."

"You going to be able to help hay the cattle again tomorrow if Delgado doesn't make it in?" Wyatt asked.

Pausing with his hand on the doorknob, Ryder looked back over his shoulder. "Sure. No problem."

"I can help, too," Jeri put in, thinking that she could make up a bit for the earlier "accidents," but to her relief Wyatt shook his head. She was finding it more and more difficult to live with the pain and inconvenience she'd inflicted on Wyatt and Ryder, even the truly accidental portions.

"Ryder and I can handle it. There's just that one little section left."

"Let Ryder heal up," Jake put in. "I'll help you, but let's get an early start."

"Deal," Wyatt agreed.

"Thanks," Ryder told them, opening the door. "I'll have everything ready for you. Call me if anything comes up with Tina."

"She'll be fine tonight," Wyatt assured him, "and we've got Jake and Kathryn here if we need them. Just get some rest. And say a prayer for her."

"Continually," Ryder promised, going out and pulling the door closed behind him.

Jeri remembered how naturally he had bowed his head when Wes Billings had prayed for Tina earlier. That could all be for show, but the Smiths seemed to be a sincere, praying family, more so than her own. She couldn't remember sitting down to pray with her family since her stepdad's death. Jeri realized that she had kind of fallen out of the habit of praying at all, and she wasn't sure why that was.

When she could, she caught the Cowboy Church services that were so prevalent at rodeos these days, but her heavy schedule didn't often allow for worship attendance. Somehow, she'd let the lack of church at-

tendance spread into a lack of prayer. Only since Bryan
had died had she started talking more to God. Most
recently, she'd asked God for a plan, a way to make
Ryder Smith pay for her brother's death. Soon after,
she'd come up with this idea.

That meant God was on her side. Didn't it?

She had to believe it did. That being the case, she
figured she'd better make the most of this opportunity.

No matter how little the idea appealed at times.

Chapter Five

With Ryder gone, Jeri, too, retired. It had been a long, strange, active day, and had included a heaping helping of anxiety due to Tina's situation. As she climbed the stairs, it occurred to Jeri that she had no plans for tomorrow, and she couldn't very well lurk around the place hoping to bump into Ryder. She needed to advance her cause, and to do that, she had to come up with a reason to spend time with him.

Maybe she could ask him to drive her around the area to look at properties? But after today, she worried he'd just send her to a local real estate agent. The local agent, however, most likely wouldn't have snow chains. After some consideration, Jeri came up with the idea of leaving a message with a local Realtor, asking for a callback during the breakfast hour, when she would be with the Smiths. That would at least lend credence to her cover story, and maybe Ryder's sense of chivalry would again induce him to offer to drive her around in Jake's truck. It wasn't exactly the most brilliant scheme, but she couldn't think of any other way to finagle a significant block of time with him.

She went online with her cell phone to identify the only local Realtor. Expecting to reach an answering service or machine, she put in the call. To her shock, a man's voice answered immediately.

"War Bonnet Realty. This is Abe Tolly. How can I help you?"

Shocked to find herself speaking with a real person, Jeri floundered a bit. "Oh, uh, I didn't expect to reach anyone this time of night."

"The beauty of cell phones," Tolly told her cheerfully. "The office goes where I do."

"I suppose that's true. Um, my name is Jeri Bogman, and I'm…raising horses, so I'm looking for someplace to do that. Property, I mean."

"I've been selling property in Oklahoma for nigh on forty years," he told her then enthusiastically began listing properties that might meet her needs. Surprisingly, he served a very wide area of the state. "Where are you located now?"

"I'm staying over at Loco Man Ranch."

That seemed to thrill him. "Excellent. Why don't you come on over to the office in the morning, say about ten? I'll show you what's available, and we'll figure out which direction we want to go in."

Suddenly, everything was moving faster than she'd anticipated. Her mind whirling, Jeri stammered, "T-Tomorrow? What about the r-roads?"

"Aw, they'll be clear by morning. By ten for sure. If not, we'll reschedule."

She didn't know what else to do but agree. "A-All right."

"Our office is between the post office and the grocery store. Can't miss us."

"Right. Okay."

She ended the call feeling uneasy. She needed to put on a good show, but she hated to waste the Realtor's time. Yes, she truly did want to start a breeding ranch but not anywhere near the Smith family. Why hadn't she realized that was going to happen? And how was she going to stall until she got what she needed from Ryder? She could turn down every property, of course, but that would just oblige her to leave the area when the Realtor ran out of options. Pondering the dilemma, she began to get an idea.

She quietly ran down the stairs and found Jake and Kathryn turning out lights in the kitchen.

"Would you mind giving me Ryder's phone number? I'd like to ask him a question before it gets too late."

Jeri punched the number into her phone as Jake rattled it off then hurried back upstairs to make the call.

Ryder answered on the third ring. "Hello?"

She could hear water running in the background. "It's Jeri. I hope I haven't caught you at a bad time."

The water shut off then. "It's fine."

"I was hoping you could do me a favor."

"Uh, sure. I'll try."

He sounded surprised, and she couldn't blame him for that, given her hot and cold behavior.

"I have an appointment with a Realtor tomorrow, and I was hoping you'd go with me. He's an older man, and I'm not sure he'll take me seriously if I'm alone."

"I expect you can hold your own, but it's probably wise for someone to go along, especially if the roads are still bad."

"That's true. Besides, you know more about this area than I do."

"Not really," Ryder said. "We haven't even been here a year yet, but I'll tag along for the meeting if it makes you feel better."

Relieved, Jeri agreed that they'd take care of the horses, his and hers, before leaving to keep her appointment. After ending the call, Jeri lay back on her bed with a smile of satisfaction. This could work out better than she'd realized. If Ryder exploded at her or made a confession in private, it would be his word against hers. And she didn't think she could trigger him into an eruption of anger in front of the family he adored. It was altogether better for a completely disinterested party to witness the same. Now, all she had to do was trigger Ryder's temper in front of the real estate agent.

For a moment, she felt a biting regret at what she had to do. If only he wasn't being so sweet about everything. But then she remembered what her brother had told her about Ryder.

"He comes off as the nicest guy you'll ever meet, but no one should be fooled. They don't call him Dark Rider for nothing. He's the most lethally gifted fighter I've ever seen."

She could still hear the admiration in Bryan's voice. Lethal admiration, as it turned out.

Deadly.

She must never forget that.

"I think you'll agree there's good grazing on this parcel," Abe Tolly said, detailing the property's finer points as enthusiastically as he had the other two they had seen. A tall, cadaverous man with salt-and-pepper hair under his cowboy hat, he fit the cowboy archetype…until he opened his mouth and waxed eloquent on soil types and pasturage.

Given the way the morning had gone, Ryder couldn't imagine why Tolly would assume Jeri would agree with anything.

As expected, Jeri leaned close to Ryder and muttered, "If you consider dead plants good grazing."

Ryder stifled a sigh. It was winter. Naturally the grass was brown and drooping, but Wyatt said weeping love grass was good grazing so long as it wasn't overgrazed in the fall. Clearly this pasture hadn't been grazed in a while, but that apparently made no difference to Jeri.

So far, she'd found fault with every property they'd seen, from the proximity to neighbors to the kind of trees on the property. Post oak, it turned out, was the least desirable of the oak species. Yet, when Ryder dryly asked which of her horses objected to post oaks, she'd burst out laughing.

Abruptly declaring herself ravenous, Jeri turned to Mr. Tolly. "I think we'll have to call it a day. I need to think about what I've seen thus far and figure out which direction to go from here, and I just can't think when I'm this hungry."

Tolly smiled politely, but Ryder wouldn't have blamed him for being put out. After all, he'd offered to buy their lunch more than an hour earlier as they'd driven right past the town. On the other hand, Ryder didn't see why the gentlemanly Realtor should have to buy anyone's lunch when he had no guarantee of making a sale. Ryder was just glad that he'd had the foresight to warn Kathryn that he and Jeri likely wouldn't be around for lunchtime at the ranch.

They rode back to town in Mr. Tolly's SUV on roads clear of all but minor patches of ice. Jeri thanked the Realtor for his efforts that morning and promised to get in touch with him again as soon as she was able.

"No problem," the older man said, shaking hands with each of them. "Y'all feel free to leave your vehicle here and walk across to the diner."

"Thank you," Ryder said, turning in that direction. To his surprise, Jeri hung back.

"Maybe you'd like to join us," she said to the Realtor. "You've missed your lunch, too. My treat." She sounded apologetic, as if she knew she'd given him a hard time.

Smiling, Tolly shook his head. "Thanks, but I have calls to make. And the diner is happy to deliver."

He pulled out his keys to unlock the door of his office. He went inside, and Ryder pointed to the diner across the street and a few yards down. Nodding, Jeri joined him, and they crossed the street. Ryder was thankful that he'd taped his toes again.

Just as he and Jeri reached the sidewalk, a tractor-trailer rig came barreling down the street and parked horizontally across several perpendicular spaces in front of the little restaurant. Because War Bonnet depended on the county sheriff's office for law enforcement, with the sheriff himself based more than thirty miles away, Ryder doubted anything would be done about it, but the driver was taking a lot for granted. Thankfully, the street wasn't exactly buzzing with activity that time of day. The dust hadn't even settled when the driver's door opened and a big, flabby fellow in faded jeans and shirtsleeves climbed down out of the cab. He smirked at them before storming into the diner.

"Boy, he's got some nerve," Jeri commented.

"Maybe he's making a delivery," Ryder said, giving the driver the benefit of the doubt.

He stepped around Jeri to pull open the glass and metal door for her, following her inside. They shed their coats and hung them on the coat rack by the door while the big trucker straddled a stool at the counter.

A small, pock-faced young man behind the counter grimaced and sighed. "Hello, Clyde. On your way to Ardmore again?"

"You know it. Where's your sister?"

"She's not here."

This information made the trucker grind his teeth. "You better not be lying to me."

"She's not here."

"You tell her I want to see her."

"She knows that, Clyde. Maybe she doesn't want to see you."

The trucker slammed a palm against the countertop hard enough to make the salt and pepper shakers rattle.

"I ain't interested in what you think about it, Nancy. Now, get my usual out here, and be quick about it."

"Name's Ned."

"I say it's Nancy."

A thin, middle-aged woman came out of the kitchen, scowling. "Why don't you try asking nicely, Clyde?"

"And what'll you do if I don't?" the trucker sneered. "Call the cops? By the time them sheriff deputies get here, I'll have this whole place busted up and be on down the road."

Scowling, the woman nodded at the boy, Ned, who brushed past her into the kitchen.

Hoping the ugliness was over, Ryder took Jeri by the arm to steer her toward a table, only to find the way

blocked by a thick leg and a dirty boot. Clyde had swiv-
eled on the stool and thrust out his foot to keep them
from passing. Ryder paused, a practiced serenity filling
him. He didn't want to fight, but he would if he had to.
Not, however, in anger. He stared silently at the brute,
who wilted a little then abruptly leaned back, bracing
his beefy forearms atop the counter.

"What's your problem, cowboy?" the trucker goaded.

Ryder said nothing. Whatever he said, the trucker
would use it against him, and silence was much more
intimidating. Realizing that he wasn't going to get a
rise out of Ryder that way, the bully dropped his leg
and switched his gaze to Jeri.

"Well, well," he jeered, "got yourself a pretty little
cowgirl, I see. Wonder if she ain't better looking without that hat." He reached out with his right hand, grinning wolfishly.

Ryder caught the man's thick wrist in midair. The
fool rocked forward as if getting to his feet, but Ryder
used his thumb to apply pressure to a certain tendon,
keeping the bully in place. His arm effectively paralyzed, poor old Clyde tried to push back, but Ryder
easily folded the other man's flabby limb against his
chest. Stymied, Clyde swung with his left fist, but Ryder
simply leaned to one side, avoiding the blow, and tightened his grip.

The man's eyes went wide, and after a moment he
gasped. "You're gonna break it!"

"Wouldn't want to do that," Ryder said calmly. "How
would you drive if I broke your wrist?"

For a long moment, the big lug just sat there, breathing heavily. Then he threw back his head and bawled,
"Forget that order!" Ryder immediately relaxed his grip

somewhat and backed up a half step. Clyde lurched to his feet, growling, "I wouldn't eat in this filthy joint if it was the only place in town!"

Ryder felt no need to point out that the diner *was* the only place to eat in War Bonnet. Instead, he said, "You'll want to leave, then." With that, he released his hold.

The big thug glared, red-faced, and stomped toward the door, shaking his hand. Ryder turned to watch him go. When the heavy glass door swung closed behind the troublemaker, Ryder turned back to the counter and the woman now standing behind it.

"Sorry about that."

"You don't have to apologize to me!" she declared, grinning. "That slug's been making trouble for us ever since my daughter refused to go out with him. It's been so bad, her little brother's been working her shift so she could avoid Clyde."

"I see. Well, if I were you, I'd call the sheriff and make a formal complaint."

"Another one, you mean. Yep, I'll do that. Maybe they'll finally track him down and put the fear of God into him."

"We can hope," Ryder said, glancing at Jeri.

Seeing her hat reminded him that he still wore his own. Lifting it off, he waved it toward a table. She pivoted and began swerving through the chairs to a spot in the corner. Ryder followed, wondering what she was thinking. She didn't meet his gaze and spoke only to the waitress. The woman left menus and water glasses, treated Ryder to another smile, and recommended the chicken fried steak.

"That'll work," Ryder said, not even looking at the menu. Jeri chose vegetable soup and a ham sandwich.

The waitress gathered their menus and hurried to the kitchen. Sitting with her hands in her lap, Jeri studied the Formica tabletop. Ryder waited her out.

After a long moment, she suddenly looked up and said, "I guess you're used to dealing with bullies."

He shook his head and shrugged. "You could say that."

Her gaze slid to the side and back again. "You ever have to do that with your brother?"

Ryder blinked and dropped his chin, momentarily puzzled. He had to think through that comment before her meaning became clear. He chuckled. "Are you talking about Wyatt?"

"He is the top man at the ranch, isn't he?"

"He is. So what?"

She shrugged. "He seems like he rides you pretty hard. I just can't help wondering if Jake found something else to do so he wouldn't have to put up with him."

Laughing, Ryder said, "It's not like that."

"No?"

"Not at all. Wyatt's the big brother. He's had to be in charge since he was fifteen. Jake and I were just ten and five when our mom died. Running the businesses was all Dad could manage, so Wyatt took over everything else. Eventually, he took over the businesses, too. It was a big load, and there were times when Jake and I gave him all kinds of trouble. But I've never doubted for a moment that Wyatt loves us. And we love him. *I* love him. And I'll always be grateful for everything he's done for me."

She stared at him, obviously disturbed, but she said nothing more.

When the food came, the waitress left the check

beside his plate. Ryder didn't even turn it over until they were done, but he quickly saw that they'd been charged only for Jeri's meal. Smiling, he shook his head and reached for his wallet. Jeri reached over then and snatched the small rectangle of paper out of his hand.

"I'll take care of this. You're here at my request, after all." When she saw that he'd been treated to a free meal, she frowned. "You've sure charmed that woman."

Ryder grinned. "It's always wise to get in good with the local diner waitress. Unlike old Clyde, I won't have to worry about what winds up in my food."

Jeri looked surprised. Then she burst out laughing again.

"Good point."

Ryder couldn't help liking the Jeri who laughed and bantered playfully. He decided that she'd given Tolly a hard time because she was nervous about making such a large purchase, and who could blame her? She was only interested in about a quarter section, 160 acres, but that still required a considerable monetary outlay, especially if the property had a house and outbuildings on it.

What difference did it make if she didn't find anything out here, anyway? At best, she was a temporary addition to his life, nothing more. And he'd be wise not to forget it.

They left the diner soon after finishing their meal and drove over to exercise her horses. Glad had been restless and moody that morning, much like Jeri felt now. After spending the entire morning in Ryder's company and witnessing that encounter with the hateful bully at the diner, she could use a good workout. Tending her horses absorbed her full attention, which helped clear her mind and allowed her to order her thoughts. She had a lot to consider, and it was all troubling.

For one thing, she couldn't quite convince herself that Ryder was still using steroids. True, he didn't look much different than he had more than a year ago, but the man was unfailingly calm and pleasant, whatever the provocation. That just wasn't consistent with steroid abuse. Her mom wouldn't want to hear that, though, and Dena expected Jeri to call this afternoon with an update. Jeri had to decide what to say to her mother.

After saddling Glad, she cleaned his fetlock support braces before mounting and giving him a good run. Ryder walked the mares, limping along on his sore toes. With the sun shining and the ground free of ice everywhere except in the deepest shadows, Jeri decided to leave the mares in the corral attached to the stables until evening. Ryder had checked the weather and turned out his horses that morning.

They made the short drive back to the ranch in silence. Jeri spoke briefly with Kathryn then went straight to her room and called her mother. As soon as the usual greetings were out of the way, Dena anxiously asked how "it" was going.

Jeri sighed. "He's not what I expected. I guess I pictured a selfish, egotistical maniac, but he's not like that at all. He's…quiet. Gentle."

"A quiet, gentle, ruthless murderer!" her mother erupted. "It's a front. What's wrong with you? Can't you see that it's all an act?"

"Mom, I've broken his toes. Nothing. I've interfered with his work, and he's responded with patience. I've insulted his family, only to have him laugh. I've complained about anything and everything. He just smiles in a slightly pitying way and teases me. Today, he put a bully in his place without so much as raising his voice. If that's an act, it's a good one."

"All you have to do is make him lose his temper," her mother reminded her. "Then we can file a new complaint and demand another drug test. That will be enough to get our case reopened, and finally, finally, he'll pay for murdering your brother!"

"Mom, that's not going to work. So far, nothing I've done has even irritated him, let alone sparked his temper."

"Then you aren't handling this correctly. Promise me that you aren't giving up. Promise me! For your brother."

Jeri closed her eyes. "I'll do my very best, I promise."

"Of course you will," Dena said, calming at her agreement. "You loved your brother. He deserves justice, and you'll see that he gets it. Then we can move on, you and I, just the two of us."

Just the two of them. When had it ever really been the two of them? Sometimes, it felt as if this grudge against Ryder was the only thing she and her mom had in common.

More and more, Jeri found herself envying the Smith family. The brothers shared a rare and special bond, and they'd drawn Tina, Kathryn and the boys into it with apparent ease and total acceptance. She and Bryan had been close, but they'd led very separate lives. Once, she'd approached him about traveling with her and helping her on the road, but he'd just laughed and said that wasn't for him. Her stepdad had put her on her first horse and supported her ambitions fully, but she hadn't started seriously competing until after his death. Since then, her mom had attended only those few events that were within easy driving distance and conveniently scheduled. Jeri didn't expect that to change. Ever.

Thoroughly depressed, she reminded her mother that she would be leaving soon for Sioux City and the first rodeo of the new season.

"Do you have to?" Dena pressed sourly. "I mean, is that really where your priorities should be?"

"Yes," Jeri insisted. "I have to come out of this with my career intact. Besides, I need the income. I do plan to start a horse breeding program, you know, and I've spent so much of my savings on private investigators and lawyers."

"For your brother!" Dena insisted. "He'd have done it for you."

It's not for him, Jeri thought. *He's beyond my help. I'm doing this for you.*

Sadly, Jeri was starting to wonder if it was even possible to give her mom closure on this. She now suspected that Ryder Smith would never stand trial for murder or even manslaughter. If she—who had come here so certain of Ryder's guilt—was now having difficulty believing that Ryder had intentionally killed her brother, others unaffected by Bryan's death would never believe so. Her best hope now was simply to get at the truth, but would her mother be satisfied with that outcome? Dena was so heavily invested in seeing Ryder punished that Jeri feared her mother would never be satisfied with anything less. In fact, Jeri feared that her mother would not be satisfied ever again. Nevertheless, Jeri would try.

"Okay, Mom. I'll keep digging and miss this one contest, but that's it. I've got Denver and Fort Worth this month, too. Besides, we've waited this long. If we have to wait a while longer, so be it. I can only do what I can do."

Feeling defeated and uncertain, Jeri resorted to prayer as soon as she got off the phone.

Lord, please show me how to handle this. Please help me get at the truth and set my mother's mind at ease.

Maybe then she could make her own peace with her brother's death and concentrate on the future.

Chapter Six

Jeri stayed in her room until dinnertime. Kathryn had warned that the meal would be a light one because the family attended the midweek prayer service at Countryside Church on Wednesday evenings. A light meal seemed perfect to Jeri, given that she'd had a late and substantial lunch. To the Smiths, however, a light meal apparently consisted of huge bowls of homemade chicken noodle soup, hot crusty rolls, a variety of cheeses and a surprisingly beautiful fruit salad.

"I need to freshen up before we leave," Kathryn said after she was done eating, rising to begin clearing the table.

Wyatt stopped her, taking dishes from her hands. "Leave this. I'll take care of it." Because Tina had to stay in bed, he would remain at home with her.

Kathryn hesitated, so Jeri added her voice to Wyatt's. "I'll help clean up. You go on and get ready." To Jeri's surprise, Kathryn shook her head.

"Oh, I hoped you'd go to prayer meeting with us."

Jeri didn't know what to say. She hadn't considered accompanying the family to church.

"Yeah, you should come," Ryder urged. "You've got a big decision to make. When I'm wrestling with a decision, I always ask God to make His pathway straight for me."

Jake smiled and nodded encouragingly. "It can't hurt. I mean, who can't use prayer? Right?"

"Right," Jeri agreed, deciding to attend the meeting. If nothing else, it would give her more time with Ryder.

As if he approved of the idea, Ryder reached out and briefly clasped her hand.

A jolt of *something* shot through Jeri, robbing her of breath and scrambling her thoughts. She managed to maintain a calm demeanor, but her mind raced. Part of her suddenly wanted to hide in her room until she could leave here, but the saner part realized that she needed prayer now more than at any time since her brother's death. Sanity won.

"How soon are we leaving?"

Jake checked the time on his phone then looked to Kathryn. "Twenty minutes?"

"Sounds right."

"What should I wear?"

"I'm just going to change my blouse," Kathryn said. "I'll be ready."

Jeri hurried up to her room, pinned up her hair and dashed through a quick shower before donning clean jeans and a fringed, long-sleeved suede shirt. She reached for the matching hat, then thought better of it and simply brushed out her long hair before adding a slender headband beaded with turquoise. She chose a pair of turquoise earrings and hurried downstairs. Ryder sat at the table in a clean shirt, fresh jeans and polished black boots, his hat at his elbow, watching Wyatt load the dishwasher. Jeri just looked at Wyatt, and Ryder shook his head.

"Wouldn't try it, if I was you. He doesn't want any help."

"That's right," Wyatt said. "I'll be through here in another ten minutes. It's not like I haven't cleaned many a kitchen in my day."

"And messed up a few, too," Ryder teased.

"I never noticed you showing any desire to cook for us," Wyatt retorted.

"Is that what you were doing, cooking?"

Shooting him a pointed glare, Wyatt said, "Yeah, you definitely look like I starved you."

Ryder chuckled and winked at Jeri. "What he doesn't know is that I used to eat at home and then go over to my friend Dave's house and eat with them."

Wyatt rolled his eyes. "Are you kidding? Dave's mom and I used to coordinate our menus to get some vegetables into you."

Ryder's mouth dropped open. "You're making that up."

"Nope."

Ryder shook his head. "And I thought I was pulling one over on you."

"That'll be the day."

Ryder laughed. "I pity Tyler and the twins. You've had more training than the average new dad. I'm going to have to apologize to them."

"Just don't give them any ideas," Wyatt said, his stern countenance cracking. "Like, for sure, don't show them how to build bicycle ramps taller than the car or give them the idea to jump off the carport roof with a blanket as a parachute." He shook his head. "How did you get through childhood in one piece?"

"God's grace," Ryder replied, grinning.

"Now, there's the truth," Wyatt agreed, pointing at him. Turning to Jeri then, he added, "He was always so quiet you never knew whether he was dreaming up some harebrained scheme or pondering the great mysteries of the universe. Or both." He looked to Ryder again. "I give you this, you never did things impulsively. You always thought them through, even if they were ridiculous."

Ryder shrugged. "Sometimes, even when I think things through, I get them wrong."

"Don't we all?" Wyatt asked, going back to loading the dishwasher.

Ryder said nothing to that.

Maybe he had thought through that sparring session with Bryan but then had gotten the moves wrong, Jeri thought. Maybe, if they became friends, he would just tell her what had happened the day her brother had died. The thought brought both hope and guilt. She didn't want to be unfaithful to her brother's memory or abandon her mom in the midst of her turmoil, but she simply couldn't hate Ryder, not without solid proof that her brother's death was more than an accident.

Kathryn came into the room wearing a beautifully embroidered tunic over jeans.

"That's gorgeous!" Jeri gushed.

"She made that," Jake announced proudly, following on Kathryn's heels. He had Frankie and Tyler by the hands.

While Kathryn herded everyone toward the door, Jake regaled Jeri with a list of Kathryn's talents and accomplishments. Kathryn blushed a deeper shade of pink with every disclosure, but she was smiling. Jeri felt the sharp sting of envy, both for Kathryn's abilities and for the praise that her husband heaped upon her.

When was the last time anyone close to her had praised her?

She had buckles and prizes aplenty, but her mom—and to an extent, her brother, too—viewed those as more fluff than accomplishment. Maybe that was why she worked so hard to excel at her sport.

Now, with only her mother left to notice, Jeri knew better than to hold her breath until she heard her own achievements praised.

Glancing around the auditorium at Countryside Church, Ryder nodded at several friends. Pleased that Jeri had so easily joined the family for the midweek service, he'd introduced her to everyone in the pews around them as "our newest guest." Ann Billings Pryor came from across the room to make Jeri's acquaintance. She had obviously heard about Jeri from her sister, who was married to Stark Burns.

"You're just as cute as Meri said," she told Jeri.

Cute? Ryder silently scoffed. Cute was for puppies and kittens. Jeri was more than cute. She was more than pretty. The girl was downright beautiful.

Jeri accepted the compliment, tepid as it seemed to Ryder, with a big smile. "Why, thank you. That's awful sweet of you both."

Ann laughed. "You're from Texas, right?"

"How'd you know?"

Ann pointed at Ryder. "You sound just like him."

Jeri seemed surprised. "Really? We're from two very different parts of the state."

Ryder tried to remember if he'd mentioned Houston to Jeri but couldn't recall, not that it mattered. Anyone in the family could have done so. What mattered was that she wouldn't have been in Houston during the uproar over Bryan's death, so she likely knew nothing of it. He hoped she wouldn't find out, at least not until she knew him better.

The women chatted a few moments longer before Ann rejoined her husband, Dean. Ryder followed Jeri into the pew and waited for her to sit before taking the place next to her.

"So whereabouts in Texas are you from?" he asked carefully.

"Abilene."

"Ah." Relieved but a little puzzled, he smiled. "Isn't there good horse pasture around Abilene?"

She rocked from side to side as if trying to get comfortable. "There is, but it's just about in the center of the state. I drive all over the country. Moving north will cut hours off my travel time for rodeo events."

"That makes sense. You could be even more centrally located in someplace like Missouri, though. I hear there are lots of rodeo cowboys living in Missouri because it gives them easy access to all areas of the country."

Again, she rocked. "Well, they probably don't have widowed mothers in the Abilene area."

"Gotcha. Guess she wouldn't want to come here to be close to you."

"Not a chance. We live barely thirty minutes apart now, and she acts like we're on different planets." Jeri looked down at her hands. "Then again, I don't get over to see her nearly as much as I ought to."

"Must be tough when you're always traveling."

"Exactly." After a moment, she asked, "So, what was it that brought you and your brothers here?"

He considered telling her the whole story, but he hadn't told anyone, not even his best friends here. If he wasn't going to discuss it with folks like Stark Burns, Wes Billings and Dean Pryor, how did he justify telling someone he'd known only a couple days?

He wasn't even sure where the impulse to tell Jeri about Bryan had come from. Sometimes her behavior troubled him, but she was a young woman under a lot of pressure, a top competitor in her field with weighty ambitions and important decisions to make. During her light, easy moments, she pulled him like a magnet, but then she'd go dark, as if a shadow had settled over her. He couldn't help wondering what that was about, and increasingly he wanted to bring the light back to her beautiful eyes.

He wondered what that said about him. Was he so pathetically lonely that he'd fixate on any pretty woman who came into his life? Or was Jeri Bogman truly special? He was beginning to think it was the latter.

Since Jake and Kathryn had married, his brothers had pushed him to date, so he'd taken out two different women. The dates had been pleasant enough, but the idea of either of them learning about his past had appalled him. He just couldn't imagine a woman who wouldn't have some doubt about him after she learned what had happened. How could he expect any woman to trust him once she knew he'd caused another man's death? Yes, he had been legally exonerated, but the fact remained that Bryan had died while sparring with him. If he couldn't get past that, how could he expect anyone else to?

He kept his mouth shut about Bryan, saying only, "We spent our summers at Loco Man, so our uncle left it to us."

He absently passed Jeri the typed prayer list, those needs and requests that were repeated weekly and kept on the list long-term. Then he reached for a prayer card in the back pocket of the pew in front of him. Though he knew that Jake would verbally request prayers for Tina and the twins, Ryder wrote a request to have Tina and the babies placed on the prayer list long-term.

As the pianist began to play the opening song, he took a deep breath, closed his eyes and asked God to help him accept that his life was forever altered by what had happened the awful day Bryan had died.

The family of Bryan Averrett.

The words shouted at Jeri from midway down the typewritten list of prayer requests. For an instant, her heart stopped.

The family of Bryan Averrett.

She couldn't believe her eyes. Who had made this request for prayer? And why? She shook her head. It couldn't have been Ryder. Could it? More likely it had come from one of his brothers. Or maybe one of his sisters-in-law. Even if what they were told wasn't the whole truth, they would know that Bryan had died. Still, seeing those words made no sense to her. Why would they make this public and risk the story coming out locally when they didn't have to?

The family of Bryan Averrett.

Rocked to the core of her being, Jeri tried to think. The family of Bryan Averrett was her and her mother, but the Smiths wouldn't know that without extensive searching. Dena had taken great care to hide their identities by immediately hiring an attorney to represent them and having only a death notice published, rather than an obituary. At one point, Ryder had asked their attorney for an opportunity to speak to them personally, but Dena had refused.

Jeri couldn't believe that Bryan would have chatted much about his family. He'd been at a rather self-absorbed phase of his life when he'd traipsed off to Houston to make his mark on the world. Even if he'd mentioned his mother and sister, she doubted he'd have talked about them by name. For one thing, he disliked that Jeri's last name was different from his and that her first name made everyone think he had a brother rather than a sister. Besides, if Bryan had made specific mention of her, wouldn't Ryder have at least remarked on the similarity of her name and that of Bryan's sister?

Jeri wished she'd paid closer attention to all that had been going on at the time of Bryan's death, but distance and scheduling had kept her out of the loop prior to the event—and after, everything had been blurred by a fog of mourning. She'd had to depend on her mom for information, and Dena didn't always make sense. Her anger and grief too often got the better of her.

All Jeri could think to do was to ask about the prayer request, but she had to do it obliquely. She nudged Ryder with her elbow and leaned close to share the list with him. Her nerves jangled like charms on a bracelet, but she kept her voice low and soft as she pointed to the top of the list.

"Who's this?"

"Oh, that's one of our deacons. He shattered his leg and has had multiple surgeries."

"Poor guy. And this?"

"An elderly lady in hospice. Been sick a long time."

They went on down the list. She learned about a little boy with diabetes and a girl with epilepsy, a couple who had lost their home... When they came to the pertinent request, Ryder gulped twice, before speaking in a strained voice.

"Bryan was a good friend of mine. Died much too young."

She studied Ryder's face, struck by the depth of his sadness. He looked as if he might weep. She realized that she had just stumbled on her best opportunity to hear his version of her brother's death, but she had to tread carefully here. If she pressed him on this would he become angry or clam up? She knew she had to try, but she was strangely reluctant. Then the opportunity passed when the music minister stepped up to the lectern and asked those in the congregation to rise to their feet.

Jeri couldn't deny the relief she felt, but she couldn't join in the singing. She had a rock in her gut and a lump in her throat, and her mind was whirling like a top. Throughout the remainder of the meeting, she struggled to concentrate on the spoken requests and prayers. All she could think about was how to bring up this subject again.

She hoped for an opportunity to speak to Ryder that evening, but after the meeting, everyone stood around the foyer of the church, visiting in groups. During that time, three different women pulled Ryder away for per-

sonal conversations. Smiling and relaxed, he hugged
two of the women in greeting and listened intently to
each of them. They each laughed at whatever he had
to say and glanced at his feet. He still limped a bit, so
she assumed he was telling them how he had hurt his
foot. Her face burned. Oh, how she wished she hadn't
dropped that mineral block.

The third woman shook hands with him then stood
there, clasping his hand and batting her eyelashes at
him. Ryder seemed a little embarrassed, but he nodded
and took out his phone. It looked like the brazen hussy
was giving him her phone number!

Ann Pryor nudged Kathryn, nodded at the pair and
muttered, "Told you."

"Maybe he doesn't know how young she is," Kathryn whispered.

Jeri couldn't help herself. "Just how old is she?"

"Eighteen."

Try as she might, Jeri could not keep the frown off
her face. "That's too young for him."

Ann grinned. "Oh, I don't know. Some eighteen-
year-olds are very mature. And twenty-five isn't that
old."

"He's almost twenty-six," Jeri heard herself say. The
other two just looked at her. *Well, he is,* she thought
grumpily. He'd turn twenty-six on February 2, just over
three weeks away. Only belatedly did she realize that it
might seem odd for her to know his birthdate after so
brief an acquaintance. Slinging on her coat, she muttered that she needed some air and walked out into the
cold to stand huffing clouds into the weak light of the
portico. When the door opened again, every one of the
Smiths streamed outside.

Talk on the drive back to the ranch centered around the boys, who were eager to describe a game they'd played during the children's service. Four-year-old Frankie was quite the clown, and he kept everyone laughing.

Once they reached the ranch house, Kathryn went inside to check on Tina while Jake and Frankie switched vehicles. Ryder kissed Frankie and ushered a sleepy Tyler into the house to greet his parents. Jeri followed but stopped at the door of Tina and Wyatt's bedroom. After dithering for a few seconds, she had to decide whether to hang around in the hallway until Ryder came out or find someplace else to wait. She went to the kitchen and sat down, but after a bit she heard Ryder and Tyler moving toward the staircase at the front of the house.

She hurried after them. Ryder took the boy into his bedroom, and again she found herself hanging around a hallway trying to decide whether to stay or move on. After a few minutes, Jeri went to her own room. Leaving the door ajar so she could hear Ryder step out into the hall again, she tugged off her boots and put them away. Then she picked up a brush, sat down on the side of the bed and went to work on her hair. She'd reached brush stroke number forty-five when she thought she heard a click. Pausing, she listened carefully but heard nothing.

After her usual hundred strokes, she plaited her hair then wandered out into the hall toward Tyler's room. The darkness at the bottom of the door showed her that the light had been turned off inside. Suddenly, she caught the barest hint of sound downstairs.

Galvanized, Jeri darted down the stairs and along the hallway into the kitchen on stockinged feet. Finding only an empty room, she hurried to the door and out onto the stoop. The faintest shadow of movement caught her eye. Turning in that direction, she saw Ryder passing through the circle of light at the far corner of the carport, heading toward the bunkhouse. She started down the steps before she remembered she was practically barefoot and shivering in the deep cold. Groaning, she spun back into the house and closed the door.

Rats.

She huffed an unhappy breath, rubbing her arms to warm herself. Well, there was always tomorrow. But how did she engage him? The horses seemed to be their only true connection.

Just as she was about to go back to her room, a deep voice asked, "Need something?"

Caught off guard, she jerked around to find Wyatt standing next to the table. He, too, wore only socks on his feet.

"I, uh, came down to get a glass of water," she lied, moving toward the sink. "I saw that the door is unlocked and wondered if I should lock it."

"I'll take care of it," he said.

Nodding, she opened a cabinet door, relieved to find the shelves lined with drinking glasses. She chose one and filled it with water. Suddenly thirsty, she drank that down and refilled the glass before turning to find Wyatt rummaging through the refrigerator.

"Good night," she called merrily, heading for her room.

As she prepared for bed, she planned how she could convince Ryder to talk about Bryan's death. Try as she might, however, she just couldn't imagine what Ryder would tell her. She wasn't even sure any longer what she wanted him to say. If he could be induced to speak on the subject at all.

Crawling beneath the bedcovers, she put the problem out of her mind by mentally going over the properties she'd seen that day. This would be a good place to start a horse ranch. It was impossible for her to do that here, of course, especially once the Smiths learned of her connection to Bryan, but maybe she really should think about moving to a more centrally located state. She began weighing the pros and cons of locations. Sleep claimed her within minutes.

Chapter Seven

When Jeri woke the next morning, brilliant shards of yellow-white light streamed through the cracks in the drapery. She stretched, feeling rested and at peace—until she remembered where she was and why. To her horror, a glance at the clock on the bedside table told her that she had forgotten to set an alarm.

She flew out of the bed, yanked on clean clothing, stomped into her boots, grabbed her hat and coat and ran down to the kitchen. The room was empty except for the boys, who were playing at the table, and Kathryn, scrubbing a skillet at the sink.

Glancing at Jeri, she smiled and said, "There you are. Help yourself to the coffee. Your breakfast is in the oven."

Her face flaming, Jeri stammered an apology. "I— I'm so s-sorry. I overslept."

"No problem." Kathryn wiped her hands on a dish towel and picked up a pair of pot holders. "You're our guest. Sleep as late as you like."

"I have to take care of my horses."

"Sit down and eat first."

Jeri dropped her coat and hat on a chair, poured herself a cup of coffee and sat at the table. Kathryn deposited a plate of waffles and bacon in front of her then went to the refrigerator for yogurt and berries. Fifteen minutes later, Jeri crammed the last piece of bacon into her mouth, swiped her face with a napkin and reached for her coat and hat, having learned that Ryder was at the shop with Jake and Wyatt had driven Tina into Ardmore to see her ob-gyn.

Jeri went out to find that the weather had turned mild. It was a good day for a ride. Questioning Ryder would just have to wait.

After driving her truck over to the Burns place, she fed the horses and saddled Betty then turned the other mares out into the corral. After stretching her own taut muscles, she mounted up and gave Betty a good run, or as good as she could, considering the limitations of the property. She returned the horse to the stables and groomed her before leading the other mares back to their stalls so she could let out Glad. He rolled in the dirt and kicked up his heels while she finished her chores.

Jeri wished there was room at the Burns compound for her to set up her barrels. It wasn't good for the horses to go days without training. She just didn't see any place level enough and big enough on the property outside of a fenced paddock behind the Burns house, where they kept their personal mounts.

Returning to Loco Man hours after she'd left, she found Ryder, Kathryn, Tina and Wyatt sitting around the kitchen table. Wyatt held his wife's hand as tears dripped from her chin.

Alarmed, Jeri asked, "What's wrong?"

Tina waved her free hand and shook her head. "I'm just frustrated."

"The doctor says she has to stay in bed for the foreseeable future," Ryder explained.

Kathryn rose to bring Jeri's lunch. She was late to the table again.

"I'm bored stupid and getting fat," Tina wailed, as Wyatt patted her hand.

"You're not getting fat," he consoled.

"I will," she insisted, sniffing. "How am I supposed to get any exercise?"

Without even thinking, Jeri said, "If you like, I'll teach you the conditioning stretches I use. I've done them for years. Many of the racers use them to stay toned and keep from getting saddle sore. You can do several in bed."

Tina's eyes brightened. "If you're any example, they must really work."

"Why, thank you."

"Better than nothing, at the very least," Ryder pointed out, smiling.

"Whoa," Wyatt cautioned. "We'd better check with the doctor first."

Tina rolled her eyes, but then she pulled a phone from the pocket of her jeans and made the call. Jeri sat down at the table next to Ryder as Kathryn brought her a plate of food. After several minutes of being switched from one person to another, Tina finally got to a nurse and explained why she was calling. A brief conversation ensued before Tina, surprisingly, passed the phone to Jeri.

Caught off guard, Jeri dropped her fork with a clank, bobbling the little phone, but then she introduced herself to the nurse on the other end of the line. What followed was nothing short of an interrogation, with Jeri describing every position and stretch. Finally, the nurse said, "She can do any of the stretches that can be performed while she's on her back or side but nothing that requires her to be on her feet, and someone should be with her while she does them."

Jeri repeated the instructions for the benefit of everyone at the table and passed the phone back to Tina. After several more moments, during which Tina brightened considerably and Jeri finished her lunch, the call ended.

"She thinks this might actually be helpful," Tina said. "So what are we waiting for?"

Realizing that she'd just volunteered herself to become Tina's physical therapist, Jeri had a moment of doubt, but then she remembered that one of her toughest competitors had maintained this workout during her own pregnancy and come out of it sleek and trim.

"You should change into something more comfortable and flexible than those jeans before we start."

Wyatt frowned, but he got up to assist Tina to her feet, saying, "I'll help you."

He shot Ryder an inscrutable glance before walking Tina to the bedroom, Tina grumbling the whole way that she wasn't an invalid and wouldn't break. Jeri began mentally planning the session.

Interrupting her thoughts, Ryder said, "I know you'll take every precaution with her, but bear in mind that she shouldn't have too much physical exertion."

Jeri knew what he was thinking. After the stunts she'd pulled that first day and dropping a fifty-pound block on his foot, she couldn't blame him or Wyatt for being uneasy about trusting her with this.

"It's just gentle stretching and holding in place," she told him. "My first trainer taught me the routine when I was twelve, and I've used it ever since." Lately, though, she'd been a bit remiss in performing the entire routine of stretches, so this would be good for her, too.

"Maybe I should learn them, too," Kathryn said. "Then I can help her when you leave."

"That's a good idea," Jeri agreed, but a dark cloud settled over her with the thought of leaving Loco Man Ranch for good.

How silly. Once she got the truth from Ryder, she'd want to leave, the sooner the better. She wouldn't want to be anywhere near here when the story broke, as it inevitably would. Her mother would never be satisfied with just learning the truth. She'd want the world to know, preferably from Ryder's own mouth in a court of law. That cloud got darker and heavier.

When Wyatt returned to say that Tina was ready, Jeri and Kathryn followed him into the spacious bedroom, where she removed her belt and boots before lying down on the floor where Tina could see her. Well aware of Wyatt hovering nearby, Jeri concentrated on making slow, easy motions, explaining each move. After she'd demonstrated each stretch, she got up and went to help Tina achieve the right poses and pressure, just as her old instructor had done for her.

At one point, Tina said, "Oh, I already feel better. I didn't realize how tense I was. God bless you, Jeri. This is a great help."

Jeri couldn't even hope that Tina would feel the same way once everyone knew about her connection to Bryan. Who, she wondered, was truly living a lie, Ryder or her? After the session, she headed to her room, only to bump into Ryder in the hallway.

He caught her by the shoulders, smiling down into

her face. Warmth flooded Jeri. Then he slid his arms around her and pulled her against his chest. Her cheek came to rest against his collarbone, the top of her head fitting neatly beneath his chin.

"Thank you," he whispered, briefly tightening the hug.

Jeri closed her eyes, impressions swimming through her. *Strong. Safe. Exciting. Right.* This, she knew instinctively, was what being held by a man should feel like. She'd never had much time to date, and she refused to indulge in the casual intimacy that sometimes surrounded the rodeo world, but she'd had a couple semiserious relationships, and she'd never experienced anything like this. She almost felt drunk with sensation, and that terrified her.

Breaking free, she fled to her room and immediately called her mother. Dena seemed testy and impatient until Jeri explained about finding the prayer request for their family the night before. At that, Dena's attitude changed.

"Smith's guilt must be eating him alive," she crowed.

Jeri hadn't even considered that. She decided not to mention what Ryder had said about Bryan being his friend and dying too young. Instead, she promised to find a way to bring up the subject again soon and get a confession out of Ryder. Then she changed the subject to Tina and how she'd helped her perform some stretches. That did not please Dena at all.

"What are you thinking? Those people are our enemies."

"They're not all our enemies, Mother. Tina wasn't even part of the family when Bryan died."

"You're getting too close to them," Dena insisted. "They're not your friends."

They felt like friends. They had been nothing but kind to her, and Jeri knew that she would go on assisting Tina in any way that she could. But then she closed her eyes, remembering what it had felt like to be held by Ryder, and she knew that she had to finish this and get out of here. The sooner the better.

She just didn't see any way to do that now without breaking her own heart.

Jeri slowed her truck and pulled it over to the side of the narrow road behind Abe Tolly's SUV. Why she had insisted on driving her own vehicle to view property this time instead of riding with Tolly, Ryder couldn't imagine. Unless it was to question him about Bryan's death, which she had been doing for some time now.

The conversation made Ryder sick to his stomach. He wished he'd never told her about Bryan, wished he'd denied even knowing him. Her curiosity was understandable, but her insistence seemed excessive. Once she knew the truth, she would undoubtedly feel nothing but disdain for him, so why not just get it over with? Try as he might, however, he couldn't seem to find the words.

"So what sort of accident was it?" Jeri asked, her dainty hands locked around the steering wheel.

Ryder sighed internally and rubbed a forefinger over his eyebrow. "A heartbreaking accident," he answered, hoping she'd take the hint. She did not.

"I don't understand."

Ryder shifted in his seat. "Neither do I. I've asked God why it happened a million times. All I can figure is that, for me, at least, it's just something I have to accept."

"And have you?"

"Not really. But I'm working on it."

"And you think that's all there is to it? You just accept and forget?"

He frowned at her. Was she serious? "I didn't say anything about forgetting. Accept that it can't be changed, yes. Forget? Never. I'll never forget. I couldn't even if I wanted to, and I don't. He was my friend. What else can I do except remember him?"

She spread her hands. "Well, there's…justice."

"There's no justice to be had in this case," Ryder pointed out, feeling drained. "It was an accident, a horrible accident that can't be undone, not by refusing to accept the reality of it or by trying to forget it—if such a thing were possible—or by assigning blame."

"But if you could undo it…"

"I would. Of course, I would. In a heartbeat." He rubbed his forehead, pulling up memories he could give her without betraying his friend. "I hadn't known Bryan very long, but I liked him, and I wanted to help him. He had dreams. You know about that, right? You couldn't have accomplished what you have if you hadn't started with a dream. Well, he had dreams, too, and he went about making them come true the best way he knew how. It might not have been the way I would do it, but he was young and headstrong and eager…"

"What do you mean, not the way you would do it?"

Ryder wished he could call back those words. He and his brothers had decided at the very beginning that nothing would be gained by blackening Bryan's reputation. He certainly wasn't going to tell this curious woman that Bryan had been involved in illegal behaviors—or that he should have done more to stop the kid. At the

time, he'd told himself that he had no proof, only suspicion, but that didn't make him feel any better now.

With great relief, Ryder saw that Tolly was striding
toward them. "There's the Realtor."

For a long moment, Jeri just sat there, staring at her
hands as if arguing with herself. Then she got out of the
truck to greet the patient, affable Realtor. After a moment's discussion, both Jeri and Tolly walked toward
the truck. Apparently, they had agreed to use Jeri's truck
for today's expedition. Ryder hopped out and offered the
front seat to the older man, but Tolly waved Ryder back.

"No, no. You're fine."

Ryder opened the back door for the Realtor and
started around to open the door for Jeri, too, but she
was already back behind the wheel. He closed the door
on the Realtor and returned to his own seat, determined
to take careful stock of the properties they would see
today.

If Wyatt ultimately decided against sponsoring the
horse business at Loco Man Ranch, Ryder reasoned that
he could always go out on his own. In fact, it might be
best if he did. He had a little money put aside but not a
lot of credit. Maybe he ought to buy that new truck now
and start building his credit rating so he could qualify
for a decent mortgage.

As directed, Jeri entered the pasture via a nearby cattle guard, and the truck bounced across sandy ground
with good grass. It looked like excellent horse country
to Ryder, but Jeri murmured about the lack of imme-
diate water. When the Realtor explained that a creek
ran nearby and windmills pumped in three other locations, Jeri merely nodded. After viewing another property, this one cut by gullies and littered with mounds

of dangerous coils of used barbed wire, they returned the Realtor to his vehicle.

"Thanks for meeting me," he said, smiling.

Ryder felt sorry for the man. Surely he felt Jeri's ambivalence as keenly as Ryder did.

"You've given me a lot to think about," Jeri said. "That last property is the most promising we've seen."

"We're making progress then," Tolly declared, getting into his SUV.

"What do you suppose that piece will go for?" Ryder asked.

Tolly considered and answered, "Two hundred thousand or thereabouts."

Ryder nodded but said nothing as he and Jeri walked back to her truck, his mood about as low as his feet. The idea of a $200,000 price tag for 160 acres with no buildings on it shocked Ryder. Admittedly, the price was cheaper than either Wyatt's or Jake's house in Houston, but Ryder hadn't owned a home to sell before making this move. He'd just have to keep saving.

At least his toes didn't throb with every step today. Another part of him did ache, though. His heart ached because his dream seemed as distant as ever and at some point he was going to have to satisfy Jeri's curiosity.

He told himself neither problem really mattered in the long run. He'd eventually get that horse ranch, and she was never meant for him, anyway. If he'd harbored unrecognized hopes in that direction, they'd been dashed as soon as she'd brought up Bryan's death. As beautiful as Jeri was, as much as she drew him, as strong as their common interests were, and as perfectly as she fit against him and felt in his arms, the two of them had no future together. Even if she permanently moved to the area, no romantic attachment could develop between them. She was already disturbed by Bryan's death. Once she knew the full story, she would be appalled.

The only mystery was why he felt so bereft, as if he'd lost something important when he'd never had it to begin with.

Jeri smiled at Ryder, who sat at the kitchen table the next morning nursing a cup of coffee. Freshly shaved and smiling, he was devastatingly handsome. She'd realized yesterday that she'd pushed too hard. Discussing Bryan's death had left her sad and edgy. She could imagine how Ryder must have felt. No wonder he hadn't confided in her. If she was too aggressive, she'd drive him away—which would accomplish nothing. As much as she wanted this fact-finding mission behind her, she understood now that she couldn't rush it. She'd simply have to wait until he trusted her enough to explain what had happened with Bryan.

Thus far, he'd revealed a deep sadness and obvious regret but not guilt. Worse, he'd implied some secret about Bryan's behavior, which meant she had to keep digging, just not so blatantly. Besides, she couldn't be displeased about spending more time in Ryder's company.

"Any chance you're free this morning?"

He shook his head. "Sorry, I've promised to help Jake right after breakfast."

Jake walked into the room just then, as if saying his name had conjured him.

"Speaking of breakfast," Kathryn said, pulling two big pans from the oven. "It's ready."

"Let me help," Jeri offered.

"You can get the oranges out of the refrigerator," Kathryn directed, transferring food onto a plate. She smiled at her husband. "Sweetheart, would you round up the boys, please?"

He strode toward the staircase. "Call me sweetheart, and I'll do anything you want."

Blushing, Kathryn giggled. They were such a cute couple. Jeri shared an amused look with Ryder, who winked at her. A swirl of pleasure sent her heart racing. Oh, if only he had never crossed paths with her brother, she thought wistfully.

"Might you have time to help me set up a practice area later in the day?" she asked, hoping she didn't sound as breathless as she felt.

"Sure. Be glad to. I'm curious about what you do, anyhow."

That should not have pleased Jeri, but it did. She couldn't quell a bright smile as she hurried to the refrigerator and took out a big bowl of quartered oranges. When she set them on the table, Ryder looked up at her.

"Is right after lunch okay?"

"Excellent."

Kathryn slid a tray filled with two plates of food onto the end of the table and reached for the orange sections. After filling a small bowl with oranges, she picked up the tray again, obviously intending to carry it in to Tina and Wyatt. Ryder immediately got to his feet.

"Here, let me do that." He took the tray from her hands and carried it toward the hallway.

As soon as he was out of earshot, Jeri turned to Kathryn. "Can I ask you something?"

"Sure."

"What happens when Ryder loses his temper?"

Kathryn pulled back so sharply that her chin almost disappeared into her throat. "I don't think he has a temper. I've never seen any sign of it. Jake, now, he can be irritable at times, but I've never seen him or Ryder act truly provoked. According to Tina, Wyatt's got a bit of a temper, but he keeps it tightly reined, and it's all over in a flash. None of the Smith brothers have any anger issues, but especially not Ryder. Why do you ask?"

Shrugging, Jeri mumbled, "Just curious. He seems extremely…even-keeled, almost unnaturally so." A sudden thought hit her, and she blurted it before she could stop herself. "Does he take medication? Mood stabilizers, maybe?"

Kathryn burst out laughing. "No way. Jake says Ryder was appalled by the heavy drug use in—" She abruptly broke off and shook her head. "Ryder doesn't like drugs of any sort. We can barely get him to use over-the-counter stuff."

Jeri wanted to press her on that, but Kathryn went back to the stove, effectively closing the subject. Besides, Jeri was beginning to think that Kathryn's assessment was entirely correct.

But what did that say about Bryan's death? Had it truly been nothing more than an accident? She couldn't quite believe that. But she couldn't quite blame Ryder anymore, either.

She just didn't know what to do or think now.

One thing seemed certain: she was going to spend more time here than she'd hoped.

Now, if only she could be unhappy about that.

Chapter Eight

Shaking his head, Ryder leaned back against a post and crossed his arms.

Jeri was at it again, asking questions. At least they weren't about Bryan's death this time. Kathryn had quietly confided that Jeri had even asked her if he had a temper and how he maintained his "even keel." To shy, careful Kathryn, the questions had somehow felt ominous, but Jake had laughed off her fears.

"The girl is sweet on him. She's looking for a way to his heart. That's all."

Silently thrilled with the idea, Ryder had made a scoffing sound and left them to meet her. Now he wondered who had been right, Kathryn or Jake? Most likely neither. Stupid as it was, though, he hoped Jake had the right of it. Not that Jeri would have to look very hard to find a way to his heart. He was already half in love with her, questions and all.

"Everyone has regrets," he told her in answer to her latest query.

She leaned against the top rail of the stall gate, reaching over it to pet Dovie's muzzle. "Oh? And what's something you did or said that you regret?"

Ryder indulged in a moment of introspection and came up with an acceptable answer. "When I was about twelve, I told my dad that he needed to get over my mother's death."

Blinking, Jeri straightened. "I can imagine how well that went over."

Ryder smiled wryly. "I was small when she died, and I remember it was an awful time, but my life wasn't so rough after that, thanks to Wyatt and Jake. In fact, by the time I hit middle school, everyone seemed fine to me, like we'd all moved on. Everyone but Dad. I'd heard Wyatt and Jake say that he just couldn't get over losing Mom, so in my great, preteen wisdom, I thought I'd let him know he needed to clean up his act."

"Oh, wow."

"Yeah. He told me that he hoped I'd love someone someday the way he loved my mom. And that I'd never have to mourn her or learn to live without her. Then he hugged me." Ryder held his thumb and forefinger about a half inch apart. "I felt about this big."

Jeri's eyes glistened dangerously, her chin wobbling as if she might cry. "That's so sad."

Ryder took a chance and slid his arms around her, pulling her close. "At least I learned an important lesson. When I told Wyatt about it, he advised me to start praying for Dad. Soon, instead of resenting him for his constant sadness I could concentrate on loving him through it. He never really got over her death, but he did seem to have more moments of joy."

Sweeping off her hat, Jeri tucked her head under

his chin and snuggled against him, her delicate hands folded against his chest. "I'm glad about that."

"Me, too."

It seemed to be his day for taking risks, so he curled a forefinger beneath her chin and turned up her face, letting his gaze fall on her lips. He gave her ample time to pull away before he tilted his head and lowered it. Before their lips met, a gust of hot breath sent his hat tumbling. He instinctively ducked. Jeri spun around and shook a finger at the pregnant mare. Dovie snorted and blew insistently.

"Cut it out! You're staying here. No matter what you do."

Ryder laughed and retrieved his hat. "She's as bad as Pearl."

"She wants to be out there with the other horses, but if I let her into the corral then don't work her, she's liable to kick the fence down." Jeri slapped her hat onto her head and folded her arms. "She's not leaving this stall until after practice."

Turning, Ryder rubbed the mare's nose. "Getting left out is no fun, is it, girl? A lady can be forgiven a fit of temper when she's expecting and locked up." He turned a grin on Jeri. "Sounds like my sister-in-law."

"I'm sure Tina would love to know she's being compared to a horse."

Still grinning, Ryder shrugged. "Just seems like we're surrounded by restless expectant mothers these days."

Jeri laughed. "That much is true. Honestly," she went on, "Dovie's the one that most loves to race, but she's had her day. Glad's the fastest. Star takes the barrels better than any of the others, but Betty's the most teachable. She's really bright."

"You can get back at it after this baby comes," Ryder crooned, scratching Dovie's chin, but Jeri shook her head.

"Actually, her racing days are over. After she foals in May, I'll take her on practice runs just to make her happy, and I might use her for instruction, but she'll never compete again. Her babies, though, that's another matter entirely. I can just imagine a horse with her love of racing and Glad's speed. What a winner that would be."

"We'll just have to pray that way, then," Ryder said.

Jeri gave him the oddest look. "You'd pray about something like that?"

"Of course. I've always believed we should pray about everything. That's how I was raised."

Jeri began stroking the animal again. "Did you hear that, girl? We're sure to get a winner now."

Jake often teased that Ryder treated the horses on Loco Man Ranch like pets. Well, if Jake was right, Ryder mused, then Jeri treated her horses like people.

"Maybe we'd better get to it," he suggested. "Every minute we stall is another minute of frustration for Dovie."

"Okay, let's get those barrels out."

They left Dovie stomping and clomping in her stall and went out through the corral to place the empty fifty-five-gallon practice barrels in the paddock behind Stark's house. As they walked the ground, though, Jeri shook her head.

"I thought I could find a way to make this work, but I can't get a full pattern on the ground here. The standard arena is a hundred and thirty feet wide and two hundred feet long. That lets you place the barrels a safe twenty-five feet from each side. This space is large enough, but part of it's too sandy and part of it's too hard. Even if we reduced the size of the pattern, I'd risk injuring my horses."

"What are you going to do?" Ryder asked.

"Only thing I can. Set up a single barrel on a sixty-foot measure and practice circles. The key to a good run is turning a tight circle, at speed, around each barrel. But tipping one adds five seconds to your time or disqualifies you."

"I see. So, where do you want the barrel?"

She trudged around for several minutes then pointed. "Ground's best through here."

Ryder rolled a barrel over and set it upright. She pulled a measuring tape from her coat pocket and handed it to him then pointed toward the corral.

"Now, we measure sixty feet straight west. Since we can't set up the whole pattern, there's no reason to set up the timer."

"Timer?"

"Sure. We use an electric-eye timer these days. You didn't think we still used stopwatches, did you?"

"Hadn't thought about it at all," Ryder admitted, studying the tape measure. The clever thing had a compass on it. "Straight west it is."

He held one end of the metal tape to the barrel while she paced off the required sixty feet, pulling out the tape as she went. Using her heel, she scraped a mark about six feet long on the ground and went to tighten Gladiator's saddle. Ryder rolled up the tape and followed her. While she warmed up Glad, Ryder saddled Star then climbed up on the paddock fence and took a seat on the top rung. It was a bright day, not uncomfortably cold despite a steady breeze. He noticed that Jeri had unzipped her jacket. She positioned Glad some fifty or sixty feet behind the starting line.

Glad danced excitedly then calmed, his hindquarters quivering. Suddenly, Jeri heeled him, and he took off like he was shot out of a cannon. Ryder gasped. They flew past the starting line and a heartbeat later were turning around the barrel. Then they were flying back the way they'd come. She slowed the stud and walked him back to position. Ryder had to laugh. If he'd ever seen an animal happy to strut his stuff, it was Gladiator. If he could have spoken, that horse would have been crowing, "Look at me! Look at me!" Star and Betty, meanwhile, stood placidly in the corral while Dovie bumped around in protest inside the barn.

Jeri put the stud through his paces maybe twenty times. The animal had developed a habit of slinging his back feet around as he circled the barrel, but she soon quelled that with pacing and the well-placed flick of a long quirt. By the end of the session, the stud was grinding that circle with his rear legs just as he was supposed to, his head low, neck outstretched, front legs gobbling up ground.

Muscle memory, Ryder thought. It was the same way with martial arts. Practice perfected technique and programmed it into the muscles.

Jeri dismounted and walked the animal into the corral. Ryder hopped off the fence and hurried to help.

"Can you cool him down while I warm up Star?"

"You got it."

"He won't want to let you lead him at first, but just pat his neck and keep walking." She started pulling herself up into the big mare's saddle, lifting her foot high off the ground.

How such a little woman could manage even to mount such tall horses, Ryder didn't know. He walked Glad over and, reins in hand, grasped Jeri by the waist, lifting her high enough she could easily slip her toe into the stirrup. She flashed him a smile and settled into the seat. Ryder wondered how so much electricity could be packed into such a slender body, but he felt it every time he touched her, sometimes just when he looked at her. Did she feel it, too?

He led Glad out of the corral, waited for Jeri to clear the opening and closed the gate behind her, before folding up the stirrups on Glad's saddle, loosening the cinch strap and starting off. True to form, Glad dug in his heels, refusing to budge. Ryder turned back and rubbed the big bay's neck just behind the jaw. The stud sidestepped, but Ryder followed, talking softly and stroking. The stud tossed his head and started forward. Ryder walked along beside him. Only when they turned back toward the corral did Ryder move into the lead. The horse followed along obediently. Eventually, Ryder walked Glad to his stall, unsaddled and curried him. He returned to the corral and saddled Betty before walking out to the paddock to watch Jeri work Star.

The mare might not have been as fast as Glad on the straightaways, but she circled the barrel as if it required no effort at all, her turns so smooth she hardly seemed to break her stride. She, too, relished the workout. When Jeri finally returned the horse to the corral, Ryder jogged over to meet her. As if she knew her turn was coming, Betty quivered in anticipation. He repeated the process with Star that he'd performed with Glad. During her cooldown, the mare didn't balk for an instant, though she kept wanting to go faster than was good for her. If he'd let her set the pace, he'd have been running to keep up. Once he had Star stabled and brushed down, he returned to the paddock to hang over the fence, fascinated by the way Jeri worked and the varied responses of the horses. Betty was not as disciplined as Star or Glad. She wanted to throw her head and prance around the barrel, but Jeri continually redirected the mare's focus. Soon, Betty was zooming down the straightaway and rounding that barrel like the pro she'd soon be.

After the requisite runs, Jeri cooled down the young mare herself and brought her into the corral, where Ryder waited to unsaddle and start grooming the animal. Jeri grabbed a brush and helped him, saying that it helped her stretch her muscles after all that time on horseback. Glancing at his watch, Ryder yelped.

"Yow! We're going to be late for dinner!"

Where had the time gone?

Jeri grabbed Betty's reins and led her toward the barn, saying, "I'd be at this for another two hours if not for you." She turned a smile over her shoulder, her big brown eyes shining. "Thanks."

"My pleasure," he told her, following along behind her. Then he stuck his hands into his pockets and kept them there while she stabled Betty and finished up. Smiling benignly, he maintained a healthy distance all the way to the truck. As she drove them back to the Loco Man, he turned his gaze out the window. Only when they were safely inside the house, sitting down to dinner with the family, did he relax his guard. He ate and chatted and talked with the others, describing the practice session to them.

And every moment his hands itched to reach for her.

* * *

Later that night, Jeri sat at the kitchen table, her stocking feet peeking out under pajamas and a long, knit bathrobe, sipping a cup of cocoa and mulling over her afternoon with Ryder. He'd been a huge help, seeming to know instinctively what needed to be done when. She'd heard snatches of him talking to the horses.

"Should've called you Pegasus. You love to fly, don't you, boy? Keep those rear feet in line, and won't be a horse out there that can beat you."

"You're just a sweetheart, aren't you?" he'd said to Star. "Hungry to please, with the dexterity and speed to do it. Any racer would be happy to have you."

Betty got a bit of a scold but an affectionate one. "What a flirt! Showing off for everyone and everything. But you put your nose to business, my lady, and you'll be unbeatable."

Jeri had even caught him whispering to Dovie. "That's okay, big mama. You'll be back out there, and you'll have a beautiful new baby that'll set all kinds of records. Think on that."

Jeri smiled at the memories. He talked to her horses the same way she did. Being on horseback always made her feel better about everything, and she happily went over the workout with each horse in her mind. Deep down, though, she knew it was all just an exercise in avoidance. She didn't even want the cocoa in her cup, but every time she thought about trying to sleep, her mind turned to that moment in Ryder's arms when he'd been about to kiss her. Why she hadn't pulled away, she didn't know, but thank God that Dovie had saved her from making a horrible mistake. She could only imagine what Ryder's kiss would be like, but she very much feared that the real thing would be her doom.

Wyatt came into the room and smiled at Jeri. "Tina's just finished her stretches. She's doing them before every meal and at bedtime. I hope that's not excessive."

Jeri shook her head. "They're basically no impact. I can't imagine doing too many. For me, it's a matter of schedule, frankly. I simply don't always have the time to go through the full routine."

"Well, just having something to do has helped Tina immensely. Thank you for thinking of them and teaching her how to do them." He rubbed his hands together, looking around the room. "Any more of that cocoa?"

"No, but I'll gladly make you a cup. It's just a packet mixed with milk."

"Sounds better than what Tina sent me in here for. Chamomile tea." He grimaced.

"Not exactly your beverage of choice, I take it."

Smiling, he looked down at his stocking feet. "Definitely not my, ahem, cup of tea."

Jeri laughed and got up from the table. "You make the chamomile, I'll make the cocoa." She pulled another packet from the pocket of her robe. He grinned and agreed.

While she filled a mug with cold milk and stirred in the powdered contents of the packet, Wyatt dropped a tea bag into a cup, filled it with hot tap water and carried it to the microwave. By tacit agreement, they placed both cups in the oven, and Wyatt set the timer.

"That ought to do it."

While the drinks heated, he went to the pantry for honey. After steeping the tea for several minutes, he removed the bag and squeezed honey into the hot liquid. As he stirred it, he glanced at Jeri. Then he took his own drink in hand and tasted it.

"Mmm. Good."

She finished off her cup and set it in the sink. "I like it."

To her surprise, he leaned a hip against the counter and looked her square in the eye.

"Can I ask you something?"

Fearing the worst, she felt her heart stutter, but she managed a nonchalant nod. "Of course."

"Do you like my brother?"

Wishing she could derail that question, she thought about asking which brother, but that would be silly, so she took a deep breath and gave him the truth. "I do. Quite a lot, actually."

"You need to know something about him then."

Jeri's first thought was *Bryan*. Was it possible Wyatt was going to tell her what Ryder would or could not bring himself to say?

Feigning nonchalance, she rinsed her cup with cold water and left it in the sink. "What's that?"

He waited until she faced him again before he said, "Ryder's not like most men. He loves with his whole heart, his whole being. And once he gives his love, he'll never take it back, never stop. I don't think he can. Our dad couldn't."

This was not what Jeri had expected, but she was relieved for some reason. "Ryder told me about your mom and dad."

"Losing my mother killed my father," Wyatt told her. "It was a long-drawn-out death, but he always said he'd go through it all again, even losing her, for the time he'd had with her."

"Losing a mate can be devastating," Jeri said softly. "My mother's been widowed twice, and I don't think she's ever really recovered from either loss."

"That's tough. Jake's first wife died, you know, and we wondered if he would fall in love again. I'm glad he did. But there will never be a second time for Ryder," Wyatt stated flatly. "He'll get one shot at happily-ever-after. Just one. That's how he's made." Shifting, Wyatt folded his arms. "What I'm telling you is this. I know my brother, and loving the wrong woman will kill him."

So, there was her solution, Jeri thought, suddenly weary. If she truly wanted to punish Ryder Smith, all she had to do was make him fall in love with her.

And destroy them both in the process.

Jeri intentionally went down to breakfast late the next morning and ate alone. She wasn't ready to see Ryder yet, or maybe she just wasn't ready to decide what she was going to do about him. While she tended her horses, though, she realized that keeping her distance wasn't going to help, so she went back to Loco Man and searched for him. He wasn't in the ranch house, but Kathryn told her that he hadn't gone to Jake's mechanic shop that morning, so Jeri trooped out to the barn. No Ryder. That left the bunkhouse.

He answered the door wearing shorts and a sleeveless tank top, mopping his face with the towel draped about his neck. Her eyes popped at the size and definition of his muscles. Behind him stood an enormous weight machine and a treadmill crammed into what was meant to be a small living area.

He greeted her with a nod of his chin. "Hey."

"You're working out." Duh.

"Yeah. I work out every day. Well, most days. I'm usually done long before now, but I overslept this morning."

"That makes two of us." She pointedly looked behind him. "So, you walk and lift weights?"

"Run," he corrected. "I run three days a week, four miles a day, and lift three days a week. I take Sundays off."

"I guess the treadmill is the way to go with this weather."

He nodded. "No one tells you how cold it gets around here. I got the treadmill for Christmas. I like it more than I expected to."

Jeri nodded. No wonder he was in such good shape. "All I do is stretch and ride."

He smiled, his gaze sliding over her. "It obviously works well for you."

Her mouth fell open at the compliment. He seemed as shocked as she felt.

Quickly, he ducked his head and backed out of the door, mumbling, "Want to come in? The house is getting cold."

She followed him inside. "Thanks." Looking around, she thought how Spartan and utilitarian the place was. No wonder he spent so much time at the big house. "I was hoping we could come to an agreement, you and I."

"Oh, about what?"

She felt a little embarrassed about even asking, but it was the perfect solution. "You were so much help yesterday. I never realized... I mean, I've always worked alone."

"Well, you obviously know what you're doing."

"I had good instruction."

"I don't doubt it, but instruction is only part of it. You have a passion for your horses and a passion for your sport. You're obviously called to it."

"Called to it? I don't know what you mean."

He tilted his head. "Pastors and missionaries aren't the only ones called by God to a specific profession or occupation. I firmly believe that Wyatt is called to ranching. It's like everything that came before was all in preparation for now, for Loco Man. Jake, too. Wyatt was upset, worried, when Jake enlisted, but I always had a real peace about it. Whatever happened, I knew he was called to that life. He and his wife were perfectly suited for the military. When she was killed and he had to give it up to take care of Frankie, we all trusted that God was calling him to something else, and now we know what that is."

"He was called to be a mechanic?"

"Yep. And he'll do a world of good through it, too. I'm convinced of it. You don't know how many times he's fixed cars at deep discount. Or for free. That's how he and Kathryn fell in love. He rebuilt the engine of her car after he found her stranded on the side of the road."

"And you, what are you called to?" Jeri asked.

Ryder shook his head. "I don't know. I used to think…" He passed a hand over his heart. "Well. What's got me on my knees right now is the idea of a horse farm. I've been wondering, though, if it should be about raising and training horses. Maybe what I should really be thinking about is rescuing."

Blinking, Jeri gasped, "Rescuing horses?"

He nodded. "I hate the idea of any animal being put down because no one can be bothered with it anymore. A horse, or any animal, that's given what was asked of it, even if that's just companionship, should be afforded a good life to its end. Don't you think?"

Jeri sighed. This man was no killer. He might have made some wrong choices that resulted in Bryan's death, but he hadn't intentionally hurt her brother. The things he'd just said couldn't have come from the brutal murderer she'd imagined him to be.

That, or he somehow knew that rescuing horses was the unspoken reason behind her drive to establish herself and earn income.

When the time for Dovie to retire had approached, Jeri had begun dreaming about a way to keep the mare. She couldn't bring herself to turn over the horse to someone who might not take care of her and afford her the long, active life she deserved. Feeding and maintaining horses didn't come cheap, though. Jeri couldn't support more than one horse that didn't earn its keep. After all, she could only compete so many times a year, and barrel racing was an expensive endeavor. She didn't have enough property in Texas to simply turn Dovie out to pasture, and she couldn't afford to hire help, but she'd reasoned that if she could raise and train just one superior horse, she'd gain enough of a reputation to expand. That notion had given her the idea for her cover story when she'd come looking for Ryder.

What if she could actually make it happen, though? And what if she could do it without buying land? Loco Man Ranch was enormous. There ought to be a part of it that could be set aside for horses. Then she and Ryder could...

She shook her head. Even imagining a partnership with Ryder Smith was ludicrous. Insane.

Dangerous.

And oh, so tempting.

Chapter Nine

"Listen," Ryder said. "I'm going to put on warmer clothes. There's a chair in that corner. Have a seat. Back in a few."

Jeri wandered over to the chair as he left the room, fighting with herself. Deciding that Ryder was no killer was one thing; considering him as a business partner was something else entirely. Her mother would likely never speak to her again if she made such an arrangement with him. But then, her mother wasn't going to be pleased with Jeri's conclusions, anyway. Still, how could she go into business with the man responsible—even indirectly—for her brother's death?

His cell phone lay on the padded arm of the chair, just begging to be picked up. Grimacing, Jeri briefly closed her eyes. She did not want to touch that thing. She wanted, surprisingly, to simply drop this whole quest, but then she thought of her mother. Her mom was all she had left. Jeri couldn't lose her, too. Besides, if Ryder didn't intentionally hurt Bryan, nothing and no one was going to prove he had.

Groaning inwardly, Jeri snatched up the little phone

and dropped down onto the cushioned seat of the arm-chair. To her shock, the phone wasn't even locked. Who didn't lock their phones these days? Maybe this was a sign that she should keep digging.

Quickly she scrolled through his contacts. He didn't have many, and he'd nicknamed them with monikers like Trainer, Dietician, Instructor, Medic. She shared any that seemed appropriate with her private investigator, sending the contacts directly from Ryder's phone. One or more of them might have been present that fateful day, or maybe they'd heard something that could be followed up. She went on to the photos, hoping to find an unedited video of that sparring match. If she could just see the full video, she might be able to put this whole ordeal to rest.

A door opened somewhere in the back of the small building, and footsteps sounded on the bare floor. She dropped the phone right back where she'd found it. Grabbing a framed photo on a shelf in the bookcase behind the chair, she pretended to study it.

"That's my family when I was tiny," Ryder said as soon as he entered the room, wearing jeans and a long-sleeved shirt.

Frowning, she glanced between him and the photo. She saw an attractive couple standing in front of a small, nondescript house with two little boys and a dog. Thinking that one of the brothers was absent, she said, "I guess the youngest one is you."

Grinning, he walked over and tapped the photo of the woman's abdomen. "That's me right there." Jeri raised her eyebrows, and Ryder laughed. "That was taken in August. I was born the following February."

"The second," she added reflexively.

This time, his eyebrows went up.

"Uh, it's been discussed," she muttered. This wasn't the first time she'd made the mistake of revealing that she knew his birthdate.

His smile flattened. "I hope the family isn't planning anything major."

"I'm not sure what they're planning," Jeri admitted. "Don't you want to celebrate your birthday?"

"Yeah, I just don't want to make a big deal out of it."

"How come?"

Shrugging, he took the photo from her hands and ran a fingertip over the glass. "Mom always made a big deal out of our birthdays." He set the photo on the shelf and went to sit on the weight bench. "Hasn't been the same since she died."

"What happened to her?"

"She fell off a ladder while cleaning an air vent."

"My biological dad was killed in a fall, too."

Ryder shook his head. "She separated her ankle, that's all. But it was real painful, and she turned out to be allergic to the pain pills they sent home with her from the emergency room."

"Are you saying the pain med killed her?"

"That's right. Anaphylactic shock. We all thought she was resting. She died in her sleep."

"Oh, no."

"Dad blamed himself because he insisted she take the pills and get into bed while he made dinner."

"But how could he know?"

"He couldn't," Ryder agreed. "No one knew that she was allergic, not even her. I think he stopped blaming himself finally, but he never got over finding her like that."

"It must have been awful."

Ryder nodded. "I didn't see her, but I heard Wyatt say she was all swollen and blotchy. That stuck with me. As a kid, I just couldn't make myself take medicine. I still have a hard time even swallowing an aspirin."

So much for the idea that Ryder was abusing steroids. What were the odds that a man whose mom had died like that, a man who had to talk himself into swallowing over-the-counter pain relievers, would succumb to the lure of an illegal drug? Jeri just couldn't believe it.

"It's tough losing a parent. My dad died when I was a baby, then my stepdad died suddenly of a heart attack when I was nineteen."

"It's funny how…unprotected…you feel when your daddy dies, isn't it? No matter how old you are."

"Yes, it is."

"Wyatt was always there for me and Jake, but when I was little, it was Mom who made me feel loved and Dad who made me feel safe. I miss them." Ryder huffed a sigh. "Life goes on, but it's not always easy."

"No, it isn't," Jeri agreed. "I miss my brother especially." As soon as the words slid out of her mouth, she wanted to bite off her tongue.

Ryder sat up straight, his palms braced atop his muscular thighs. "Your brother died, too? I didn't know. I'm so sorry. You must've been really close to him," Ryder surmised, leaning forward again and taking both of her hands in his.

Jeri closed her eyes and felt him press her hands before nodding briskly. "I—I was."

"Oh, man. If anything ever happened to one of my brothers…" Ryder shook his head. "And your poor mom. Both husbands *and* her son. That's a lot for anyone to bear."

Looking Ryder straight in the eyes, Jeri said, "Losing him has almost unhinged my mother."

"Well, you can't blame the poor woman. Do you mind if I ask how your brother died?"

You killed him, Jeri thought, but she couldn't say that. Neither could she dredge up the rancor and anger that usually accompanied that thought.

"We're not sure," she finally said. "We just don't know."

"Oh, that's bad," Ryder commiserated, shaking his head. "I'm real sorry about that. I'll pray for you and your mom."

You already are.

The thought came with certainty. It was just about the only thing she knew for certain now, but she knew, in her heart, that Ryder Smith consistently prayed for her and her mother.

He just didn't know it.

And Jeri prayed that he never found out, for if he did, he'd surely hate her for duping him.

"Don't take too long to change," Wyatt instructed as Ryder slid out of the SUV under cover of the ranch house's carport the next day. "I'm starved."

"There's soup in the Crock-Pot," Kathryn reminded him calmly, letting herself out of the back seat. "I'll make some grilled cheese sandwiches to go with it."

"I'll get the boys changed," Jake announced.

Usually, Ryder would have been anxious to get out of his church clothes, but Jeri was in there with Tina, and he was eager to see her. Jeri had surprised him with her compassion and understanding the afternoon before, and he'd been looking forward to spending more time with her. He'd been disappointed when she'd volunteered to stay with Tina instead of attending the worship service that morning.

"This will be my only chance," she'd said, making it sound like a privilege rather than a chore. "Once I get back out on the road, I'll be competing or traveling every Sunday."

Selfishly, Ryder had hoped that Wyatt would refuse Jeri's offer, but Tina had urged him to go to church, and he'd given in.

Loosening his string tie, Ryder said, "I'll change later. After lunch. Someone should help Kathryn get the food on the table."

Wyatt traded looks with Jake, who was pulling Frankie out of his safety seat.

"Right," Wyatt drawled. "Because you're always so keen to help Kathryn prepare meals."

"He does help," Kathryn said mildly. "From time to time."

Ryder stuck out his tongue at Wyatt, who laughed. Feeling lighthearted, Ryder followed Kathryn into the house, only to bump into her when she came up short just inside the door. The acrid scent of burnt food assailed his nostrils. Jeri sat dejectedly at the table, one elbow braced on the tabletop, the other arm hanging over the back of her chair.

Kathryn put a hand to her forehead, looking around the room. The place was a disaster. "What on earth?"

Jeri flipped a hand morosely. "I followed Tina's instructions to the letter, but…" She shook her head. "I melted the butter first and I counted to ten, but the bread came up black. I tried buttering the bread. I counted to ten. Burned. I tried it without butter. Counted to six. The bread was perfectly browned, but the cheese didn't melt. So I tried another skillet. Tina went through it all with me again." She slashed a hand in defeat. "I cannot make a decent grilled cheese sandwich."

"And apparently, you can't do it without using every skillet in the kitchen," Kathryn muttered.

Ryder might have laughed if tears hadn't filled Jeri's big brown eyes.

"I don't know how you do it," Jeri admitted, her chin wobbling.

"Well," Kathryn said briskly, putting on a smile, "when you live without conveniences like fast-food restaurants, you learn to do for yourself. Or live on frozen dinners."

"I eat mostly in restaurants," Jeri grumbled. "I can scrounge a decent meal out of a convenience store in a pinch, but…" She gusted a pitiful sigh. "Not much opportunity to actually cook."

"Probably just as well," Wyatt said under his breath, pushing past Ryder. Jake and the boys crowded in behind him, prompting Kathryn to hang up her coat. Ryder ventured on into the room, carefully peeling off his overcoat.

"Don't worry," he said to Jeri. "I'll help you clean up while Kathryn makes the grilled cheese sandwiches. Won't take long."

"There's no more cheese," Jeri informed him glumly.

Kathryn paused in the act of tying on an apron, but then she gamely smiled. "Who's up for BLTs?"

"Me!" Wyatt and Tyler both exclaimed.

Jeri's chin wobbled again. "There's no more bread."

Kathryn looked stunned, but she quickly rallied. "Crackers. We'll have crackers with our soup."

"Lots and lots of crackers," Jake drawled, hanging up Frankie's coat.

Glancing at Jeri, Ryder went to hang up his coat and hat, too.

"Think I'll eat with my wife," Wyatt said from behind a smile, but Ryder recognized the tic at the corner of his eye. His big brother was holding onto his temper by a thin thread.

Jake herded the boys after him. Jeri sat slumped at the table, looking as if she'd lost her last friend.

Ryder shrugged out of his suit jacket and hung it on the back of a chair. "Don't be so hard on yourself."

"I'm a complete failure."

He chuckled, jerking his thumb at the door. "There's a fancy dualie sitting out there that suggests otherwise."

One corner of her lips curved ever so slightly at that.

"I'll teach you to cook, if you want," Kathryn said, taking soup bowls out of the cabinet.

"I'll only be here until Thursday," Jeri groused. "We could work around the clock until then, and I'd still burn the grilled cheese."

"What happens Thursday?"

"Denver."

"Oh, that's right. You told us you didn't have a lot of time to look for property because you'd be traveling to and from competitions. I guess that means rodeos."

"Mostly," Jeri said. "There are other types of competition."

"Denver is a long haul to make by yourself," Ryder worried aloud.

She shrugged. "I'm used to it. I've been doing it since

I turned twenty. Besides, I've already missed Sioux City. I have to make Denver."

"I see." He hated to think of her being on the road alone, but it wasn't any of his business. Still, he could keep track of her, at least. "You'll be back next week, though, won't you?"

"Yeah. For a few days. Then I drive down to Fort Worth. That's an easy one. It's…what? Three, four hours from here?"

"Something like that. You taking all of your horses with you?"

"Just two. Glad and Star. Betty's not ready yet, and Dovie is better off here." She sighed again. "I could sure use some practice, but I don't have any place to set up the barrels. The ground's too hard at the Burns paddock."

"You could get Dean Pryor to disc it for you," Wyatt said, returning to the room. "He'll probably do it real cheap. Or for nothing."

"I'll take you over to the Pryors' this afternoon, if you like," Ryder told her.

"Yes," she agreed, sniffing. "That would help. Thanks."

Wyatt went to pick up the tray, which Kathryn had piled with crackers and apple slices. "We've still got pound cake," she told him, "and canned peaches to put over it."

"I'll be back," Wyatt promised enthusiastically.

The boys ran into the room then, followed by Jake. Kathryn held up two boxes. "What'll it be? Animal crackers or saltines?"

"Aminal quackers!" Frankie cried.

"Both!" Tyler insisted.

"Yeah. Bof," Frankie amended.

Grinning, Jake went to gather up the plates stacked on the counter at Kathryn's elbow. "I'll have saltine quackers," he teased. Kathryn laughed. He kissed her on the cheek and carried the plates to the table to begin doling them out.

Ryder went to carry a bowl of soup to Frankie. Jeri got up and followed him to help, but when she started back to the table, hot soup sloshed over the edge of the bowl and onto the floor. She instantly burst into tears. Ryder took the bowls, placing them on the table beside his. Then he gingerly pulled her into his arms.

"There, there. It's not that bad."

"I just want to go back to bed and start this day over," she whined, huddling against him.

He smiled against the top of her head. The girl fit like she was made for him. Maybe she was. Maybe he was wrong. Maybe he and Jeri had a chance for something more than temporary friendship.

And maybe he was losing his mind.

At the moment, he didn't much care. She felt like the sweetest thing in the world, standing there in his arms, sniffling against his chest.

After lunch, he helped her clean up her mess, loading dishes into the dishwasher and wiping down the countertops and stove while she scrubbed the heavy skillets. Kathryn surmised that Jeri had overheated the skillets before browning the sandwiches. Jeri listened carefully, nodding as Kathryn quietly, gently explained the process. In the end, she promised to replace the bread and cheese, despite Kathryn's protests.

The grocery store in War Bonnet was closed on Sundays, so Ryder promised to take Jeri into Ardmore after they saw Dean Pryor. While he was thinking about it, he called Dean and asked if they could come over, but he didn't intend to ask Dean to disc up *Stark's* paddock. He already knew that space was too small.

He planned what he was going to say as he went out to the bunkhouse and changed into jeans and a sweater. When he returned to the house, he went in to speak to Wyatt and Tina. He assured Tina that Jeri had recovered from the morning's debacle before broaching the subject he'd really come to discuss.

"Listen, Wyatt, she won't say it, but that paddock over at Stark's is unsuitable in more ways than one. I think we should have Dean disc a suitable space over here. In fact, I think we should bring Jeri's horses over here. I don't want to deprive Stark of a paying customer, but we've got the room, and it would be so much more convenient over here. It would cut an hour off my own workday at least. And Tina and Kathryn are going to want the ground tilled for a garden this spring anyway. Let me tell Jeri to move her horses and practice here."

The accommodations at Loco Man weren't as luxurious as those at Stark's place, but they were more than adequate. Surely they could suit her current needs better at Loco Man.

Wyatt was lying on the bed next to Tina, atop the covers, his arms tucked behind his head, his stockinged feet crossed at the ankles.

"Have you talked to her about this?"

"No."

Wyatt sighed. "I don't know, Ryder. That girl's a walking catastrophe."

"Not in everything," Ryder insisted. "Okay, she can't make a grilled cheese sandwich to save her life, but

Rex could learn a thing or two from her when it comes to horses."

Rex was the acknowledged horse nerd in the area. As a veterinarian, Stark knew loads about horses, but Rex could spend hours on the computer researching the animals.

Wyatt rocked up into a sitting position, grinning. "And you're not the least bit biased where she's concerned, are you?"

Ryder felt his face heat, but he didn't cavil. "Maybe. But I'm not wrong. She's good."

"Okay, she's good. And?"

"We're heading over to Dean's in a few minutes. You know Dean will disc our ground for nothing if we ask. I'll put up temporary fencing myself."

Narrowing his eyes, Wyatt deliberated. "Are you sure you want to get that involved with this girl, Ryder?"

He tried to consider his answer dispassionately, but he already knew what he was going to say. "Yeah, I do. I want to help her work her horses, and that'll be easier here. For everyone."

Wyatt lifted his eyebrows then settled back onto his pillow. "Okay by me."

Pleased, Ryder couldn't catch back a sigh of relief. "Thanks, Wyatt."

Smiling, Tina smoothed the bedcovers with her hands. "She worked so hard at those grilled cheese sandwiches, but I guess I'm not the best instructor, and she threatened to call Wyatt at church if I got up to help her."

Ducking his head, Ryder smiled. Maybe she was accident prone and choosy, and she definitely could not cook, but she was thoughtful and caring. And beautiful. So beautiful.

"Dinner's on me tonight. I have to take Jeri into Ardmore, so I'll pick up some burgers, if that's all right with everyone."

The family had adopted the habit of fending for themselves on Sundays so Kathryn could have the time off at home with her husband and son, but with Tina laid up that had become problematic. Ryder figured this was the least he could do in light of Wyatt's cooperation on Jeri's situation.

"Sounds good to me," Wyatt agreed. Tina nodded, smiling.

Ryder hurried upstairs to tell Jeri that they were expected at the Pryors' and propose the new plan. When he tapped on her door, she called out.

"One minute."

He heard her speaking to someone, which meant she was probably on the phone, but he didn't even try to make out the words. After a few seconds, she opened the door. Her eyelashes sparkled, as if she'd been crying again.

"Ryder."

"You okay?"

She nodded and smiled wanly. "Fine."

He told her what he'd discussed with Wyatt. For a long moment, she just stood there and stared at him. Then her eyes began to glisten again.

"Seriously? Here at Loco Man?"

"Wouldn't that be best all the way around?"

Bowing her head, she squeaked, "Yes."

"Then why are you upset?" he asked softly.

He heard her gulp. Then she shook her head, the long, dark, glossy strands of her hair rippling.

"I'm not. I'm…" She looked up, blinking away tears. "I'm grateful. And, of course, I'll pay you what I'm paying Burns."

"We'll work that out later," he told her. "Right now, Dean and Ann are expecting us. You'll need to explain to him exactly how you need the ground prepared."

"Let me pull on my boots." She turned back into her room to do that and returned moments later, throwing on her coat.

They walked downstairs together. Ryder shrugged into his coat and picked up his hat. At the same time, Jeri thrust her keys at him.

"You drive. You know where we're going."

The Pryor farm was only five miles away and easy to find, but Ryder smiled and took the keys before grabbing an insulated bag from the top of the refrigerator. If Dean kept them talking for a while, which was very likely, they might not return to the ranch before heading over to Ardmore for the food. The insulated bag would keep the food hot on the drive back home.

It went exactly as Ryder anticipated. Billie, Dean's grandmother, insisted on serving them coffee and cookies. Ann chatted up Jeri, learning in minutes what it had taken Ryder the better part of a week to discover. Dean and Ann's kids had to introduce Jeri to their dog, Digger, who was only too happy for the attention. The Pryors wanted to know all about Tina and her situation. Then Dean questioned Jeri extensively about barrel racing. An hour passed before Ryder could get to the reason for their visit. That necessitated another discussion about preparing the ground properly for Jeri's purposes. Dean brushed off any suggestion of pay.

"It's a small job, and I'm not doing anything right now, anyway. I'll get to work on it first thing in the morning."

"And he does mean first thing," Ann warned them.

Dean shrugged. "Farmer's lot in life, rising with the sun."

"I hope it's not too cold," Jeri worried aloud.

Shaking his head, Dean said, "Working the ground'll warm it up. Lot of friction involved."

"I think she meant for you," Ryder clarified, winking at Jeri.

"Oh, I'll be inside, snug as a bug in a rug. You know, tractors have cabs these days, not just a cold metal seat. Or at least mine does." He grinned.

"A farmer's lot," Ann deadpanned, and they all laughed.

By the time Ryder and Jeri rose to leave, Billie was urging them to stay for supper.

"Thank you, but another time. I promised everyone hamburgers."

They took their leave amid hugs and invitations for meals in the future. As they walked to the truck, Jeri commented, "Life seems to revolve around food here. Have you noticed that?"

Ryder chuckled. "Yeah, I have, but when you don't enjoy the luxury of restaurants and grocery stores around every corner, you spend a lot of time planning meals and cooking them. Meals become more of a family event. I like it. But then I don't have to do the planning, shopping and cooking."

"Sure beats gobbling down junk food alone," Jeri muttered.

"No doubt," Ryder said.

Not for the first time, he thought that she shouldn't be out on the road traveling alone, but what could he do about it?

He didn't dare ponder that question for long. It was too soon for the thought circling around in the back of his mind. Too soon. Too tempting.

And far too unlikely.

Chapter Ten

By the time they hit Ardmore city limits, they'd worked out all the details of moving Jeri's horses and rig. Her excitement was palpable. Ryder didn't think he'd ever seen her quite so relaxed. Even when she called Stark Burns to tell him she'd be moving the horses, she seemed easy and certain.

"Dr. Burns didn't sound particularly surprised," Jeri reported after the phone call. "I think he might even have been relieved. He said moving the horses would make it easier for him to quarantine some cattle coming in from somewhere."

"It's all working out for the best, then," Ryder concluded.

They stopped at a grocery store and picked up bread and cheese, as well as a few things Jeri said she'd need "for the road."

He hated to think about her leaving on Thursday, alone, towing a big trailer and horses, but he didn't see what he could do about it. At least not in the short run.

After the grocery store, they went to Tina's favorite burger shop and walked inside to place the order. Ryder knew how everyone preferred their hamburgers except Jeri, so he had her order for herself, but then Jeri insisted on paying the tab, no matter how much he protested.

"I ruined lunch. The least I can do is pay for dinner."

"Darlin', it was just a few sandwiches."

She blinked at him, looking stunned. He couldn't think why for several heartbeats. Then it hit him.

Darling. Yow. How had that rolled off his tongue without him even thinking about it?

She recovered before he did. "A few?" she scoffed, looking away. "I could've eaten for a month on the left-overs. If they'd been edible."

Ryder laughed and slung an arm about her shoulders in good-buddy fashion, aiming her toward the dining area. They sat down with sodas until the burgers were ready. After carrying the paper bags of food to the truck, he loaded them into the insulated bag, all but for one burger, with bacon and extra mustard, plus a cardboard container of French fries.

Handing the keys to Jeri, he said, "You know where you're going now. Besides, I intend to eat on the way home."

"No fair," she complained, pretending to pout.

He winked. "If you're good, I'll feed you fries."

Smiling, she climbed behind the steering wheel and adjusted the seat. Then she ate every fry he offered her on the way home, which was most of them.

He was obsessed with her lips well before she pulled the truck into its customary space in the carport. He stepped into the cold evening air with a great sense of relief, and then, after he delivered the burgers, he bolted to the bunkhouse. He read late into the night, only to wake in the morning wondering if Jeri would slug him if he kissed her.

He didn't think she would, but he wouldn't put it past her. She wouldn't care a whit that he was twice her size, and his sore toes told him that she could hurt him if she wanted to.

For some reason, that made him smile.

"You pretty."

Smiling, Jeri tapped the nose of Dean and Ann Pryor's little daughter. "You're pretty, too."

Glory giggled, her bright red head bobbing. Dean had apologized for bringing her along but claimed she wouldn't be left behind. Apparently, the child was fascinated by Jeri's hair. Sitting in Jeri's lap at the kitchen table in the Loco Man ranch house, Glory repeatedly sifted the long, sleek locks through her chubby fingers. Personally, Ryder felt everyone kept underestimating Jeri Bogman. The word "pretty" didn't begin to cover her beauty. The woman was breathtaking, especially on horseback.

He filled a thermos with hot coffee and capped it, then began making another pot so it would be ready to brew when Kathryn came in.

"Let's go, curly top," Dean instructed, holding out his arms to his daughter. "We've got work to do."

Glory shoved two fingers into her mouth and shook her head. "I shtay," she insisted around her fingers.

"How about I go with you?" Jeri suggested, rising and setting the child on her feet.

Glory giggled around her fingers. "Yeth."

Jeri threw on her down coat. Ryder was still wearing

his coat. He picked up the thermos and tucked it into the crook of one arm.

"Let's get to it."

Jeri rode with Dean and Glory in his one-ton truck. They pulled the tractor and its blades out to the pasture on its trailer. While she opened and closed the gate and walked the ground with Glory to determine the best place to plow, Dean off-loaded the tractor and attached the largest disc harrow. Ryder, meanwhile, stacked as many temporary metal fence sections into the bed of Wyatt's truck as possible. Dean, with Glory in the cab next to him, was already churning up ground when Ryder arrived on the scene. Jeri hurried over to help him remove the fence sections.

They didn't have enough fencing to completely enclose the practice area, but Jeri said it would suffice.

"We'll mark off the corners and set up a small enclosure for the horses. Then we'll place the rest of the fence sections even with the barrels so the horses can see them."

"Sounds good."

By the time they got the horse pen set up, Dean was cross-plowing the initial harrows with a smaller disc. After he finished that, Ryder helped him change the disc for a landscape rake. That gathered a few rocks, which Ryder pitched to one side. A second raking left the ground loamy and soft, but Dean worried that it would soon pack down again.

"I brought a scoop for this thing," he said, patting his tractor affectionately. "Seems like I remember a real sandy section off to the east there."

Ryder knew where Dean meant. It was about a quarter mile right down the fence line. He drove the truck while Dean followed in the tractor with the scoop on the front. Dean heaped the truck bed with sand, and Ryder drove it back to the practice area. Dean grabbed a shovel, stood in the bed of the truck, and threw out sand while Ryder slowly drove around the practice ground. Then Dean raked the ground twice more. Finally satisfied, he loaded the tractor back onto the trailer. When he came to take his leave of them, Glory riding on his hip, Jeri beamed all over him.

"You could take up a sideline preparing rodeo arenas."

Dean chuckled. "I'll keep that in mind." Then he hugged his daughter. "Come on, curly top. Ganny's waiting breakfast on us."

"Ganny?" Ryder echoed.

"That's what she calls my grandmother."

"Ah. Speaking of breakfast, I saw Kathryn and Jake arrive quite a while ago." He motioned for Jeri to get into the truck. She hugged and kissed Glory first, then thanked Dean again.

"Are you sure I can't pay you for this?"

He shook his head. "I'll get you back eventually. Provided you hang around."

"She's hanging," Ryder said with more confidence than he truly felt. "She's looking at properties now."

Dean smiled. "Well, then I'll get to do this again." He doffed his hat and carried Glory to his vehicle.

Ryder and Jeri drove ahead of him to the gate and opened it, closing it again after Dean pulled his rig through. Dean waved and kept driving. Ryder and Jeri followed as far as the house, where they parked beneath the carport and got out.

Even Wyatt was at the table when they went inside.

Twisting sideways, he draped an arm over the back of his chair, looking at them.

"Well?"

Jeri smiled. "It's wonderful. I can't thank you enough."

He lifted his eyebrows and went back to his plate. "A real practice arena needs a cover. Otherwise, you'll have Dean reworking it constantly."

"I'll worry about that later," Jeri said. Ryder hung his coat on the wall, and she covered it with hers. "Right now I've got to think about getting ready for Denver." She picked an empty peg and hung up her hat. Ryder left his on the little table beneath.

"Soon as I eat, we'll take care of my horses, then go get yours," Ryder promised, ushering her toward the table.

As they sat down, Jake relaxed back in his chair, having finished his meal, and crossed his legs. Kathryn, who never seemed to sit, came over and refilled his coffee cup while Ryder and Jeri filled their plates.

"Thank you, honey." Jake looped an arm around Kathryn's waist and pulled her close, sipping his coffee. Ryder couldn't help grinning even as he tucked into his food, so naturally Jake had to tease him. "You oughta consider getting' one of these for yourself, little brother."

Ryder looked up, brow wrinkling. "One of what?"

"Wives." He looked at Kathryn, who blushed furiously and rolled her eyes. "They're sweet things to have around."

"Keep it up and you'll have hot coffee in your lap," Wyatt warned, splitting a look between Jake and Kathryn. Jeri, Ryder noticed, folded her hands in her lap and stayed silent.

"That's your wife, not mine," Jake quipped, smiling up at Kathryn.

"And don't you forget it!" Tina shouted from the bedroom.

"Remind me to close that door," Wyatt drawled, while everyone laughed. Everyone but Ryder.

Jake finally realized he might have gone too far. He sat up straight, laying his forearms flat against the tabletop.

"Hey, I'm sorry, Ryder. I didn't mean to embarrass you. I was only teasing."

"I know," Ryder said as lightly as he could manage.

"Then what's wrong?" Wyatt demanded, glancing at Jeri.

"Nothing," Ryder tried.

"Something's wrong," Jake said. It was the gentle tone that made Ryder venture an explanation.

"It's just that…after what happened, I—I don't see myself finding anyone who…" He was painfully aware of Jeri watching him. "I just don't think it's very likely that I'll marry."

"Yeah, I that thought, too," Jake drawled. "Twice. Thankfully, I was wrong both times."

"But you didn't—" Ryder broke off, because, in addition to Jeri, both boys were at the table. He could practically see their ears twitching.

Kathryn seemed to follow his train of thought. She set down the coffee carafe and pulled out Frankie's chair. "Go upstairs now. I'll bring you a treat in a little while."

"You, too, Ty," Wyatt said so implacably the boy

didn't even argue. Tyler just slipped off his chair, took Frankie by the hand and left the room.

Ryder wanted to say that the boys could stay, that the subject was closed, but he knew from long experience that wasn't going to work.

As soon as they heard the boys clomping up the stairs, Wyatt spoke again, keeping his voice low and pecking the tabletop with a fingertip for emphasis. "You did not kill that boy."

"Wyatt, please."

"And you need to stop acting like it."

"He died," Ryder whispered, "that's all I know."

"You're talking about Bryan," Jeri suddenly blurted, and Ryder squeezed his eyes closed. He had so hoped that subject was forgotten between them. He should've known better.

"He told you about that?" Jake asked. "Then you know it wasn't his fault."

"Bryan was the one who wouldn't let it go," Wyatt put in. "He was the one who insisted on trying, over and over again."

"He just wanted to break the hold," Ryder argued miserably. "I—I should've let him beat it."

"You'd never have let him go into a fight believing he could break that hold," Jake stated flatly. "As juiced up as that kid was, someone would've gotten hurt, and you know it."

"Yes, but—" Ryder began, only to have Jeri interrupt.

"Juiced up? What does that mean?"

"Steroids," Jake answered bluntly. "Lots of these young hotheads think that's the way to break into professional matches, but it actually works against them.

You've got to have a cool head to figure your way out of some situations in a fight."

"Steroids make you lose your temper," Wyatt explained. "Big muscles aren't the key, anyway. You've got to have skill and endurance, as well as smarts."

"How do you know he was using steroids?" Jeri demanded in a strangled voice.

"The autopsy showed it."

She gasped. "I don't understand."

"It's in the report. There's a whole page listing the stuff they found in his system."

"A whole page," Jeri repeated softly.

"Mostly supplements," Ryder said. He hated to hear Bryan blamed for what had happened. Bryan had died. That was bad enough without dragging his memory through the dirt.

"And a whopping load of steroids," Wyatt added doggedly. "You suspected it for weeks and talked yourself blue in the face, trying to make him see reason."

"For all the good it did," Ryder mumbled. He scrubbed a hand over his face. "I should've turned him in or refused to spar with him."

"And how would you prove he was using? How would you keep him from finding someone else to spar with? You did everything you could," Wyatt insisted.

Jeri lifted a hand to her mouth, seeming deeply moved. She took several slow breaths and asked, "What happened exactly?"

She sounded rung out, as appalled as Ryder had feared she would be. He couldn't answer her. Instead, Jake spilled the whole ugly story.

"They were sparring, practicing. Ryder was showing Bryan a new hold, and Bryan couldn't break it, no matter what he tried. He lost his temper. Ryder tried to call a halt, but Bryan was in a frenzy. Ryder tried to calm him, but Bryan maneuvered his way around until he could climb the wall, literally walked right up it, facing the ceiling, with Ryder holding his upper body."

Wyatt picked up the story. "Ryder couldn't release Bryan without dropping him, and they were off the mat, nothing but concrete floor beneath them. Bryan tried to throw himself backward over Ryder's head. His neck snapped."

"I heard it," Ryder whispered. Over and over again he heard the awful sound of bones and ligaments snapping in his dreams. How could he not? Ryder supposed that Bryan had intended to land on his feet behind him, but instead Bryan's neck had snapped against Ryder's shoulder. "He was gone in an instant. I couldn't hold him up." He'd tried. Somehow, in the moment, it had seemed that if he could just get Bryan on his feet, he'd be okay, but Bryan had collapsed like a marionette when the strings are cut.

"I suppose you can prove this," Jeri said, tensed as if she had to work to keep herself in her seat.

Wyatt responded. "We've got the tape of the practice session, almost an hour's worth, the autopsy report, the police reports, witness statements."

"I've always wondered what an autopsy report was like," she said, sounding anything but curious. "How long it might be, for instance."

"This one is several pages," Wyatt told her in a puzzled tone.

"Several pages," Jeri mumbled. "Makes sense."

"The important thing," Jake put in testily, "is that

Ryder was completely exonerated. By everyone but himself."

"You know that's not so," Ryder retorted.

"What Ryder means is that Bryan's family blames him," Wyatt explained, holding up a hand to stop the exclamation on the tip of Ryder's tongue. "Which is entirely understandable. But that doesn't mean you did anything wrong."

Jeri abruptly shot to her feet. "I should go."

Dismayed, Ryder looked up at her. Her face seemed set in stone, and his heart dropped as if it were made of the same stuff.

"I—I mean, I should get to work. We should…" Rushing to the door, she grabbed her coat and hat and went out.

Glumly, his appetite gone, Ryder got to his feet and followed, slapping his hat on his head and plucking his coat off the peg on the wall. He moved slowly, in no rush to face the woman he'd find outside. She would be cold now in a way that had nothing to do with the temperature outside. She would be stiff and unfriendly, her warm brown gaze never quite meeting his again. Deep in his heart, he lamented the loss of that impish glimmer in her eyes, the silent respect and approval as they worked the horses.

Within the space of a single breath, he stepped outside and realized how wrong he could be. She wasn't cold. She was hot, as in livid.

"Stupid, macho, selfish…"

Ryder hung his head. "I should've let him break the hold. But he'd never lost his temper that badly before. He'd get steamed, yeah, but he never went crazy like that day. I was just trying to help him learn the hold. I wasn't trying to—"

"Not you!" she interrupted. "Bryan! He took a stupid, macho, selfish risk. What about his family, the people who loved him? Didn't he think of them?"

Weak with relief, Ryder took her fists into his hands. "Don't be upset."

"It's just…" She relaxed her fingers, looking down at them. "My brother was the same way, and it cost him his life."

Ryder couldn't help himself. Dropping her hands, he wrapped his arms around her, elated when she pressed herself against him.

"Don't be mad at him," Ryder urged softly. "Young men think they're invincible. What seems foolish to everyone else often seems well worth the risk to a young fellow feeling strong and courageous."

"Not you," she whispered. "You're sensible and good."

Delighted, he chuckled. Maybe she wouldn't hate him, after all. Then he shook his head. "I was a mixed martial arts fighter. How sensible is that?"

"Not very, I guess."

"Do you know what mixed martial arts is?"

"Yes."

"Wyatt enrolled me in my first class when I was ten." She turned her face up to his. "Why would he do that?"

A grimace escaped before he could restrain it. "I was being bullied by some older kids."

"What?"

He shrugged. "I was real big for my age and clumsy. These older kids used to corner me after school. Wyatt decided I needed to learn to defend myself, and he was right.

The first time I threw one of them over my shoulder, that was the end of it. But I was hooked. I took every martial arts class I could find. And when I turned twenty-one, I let a promoter talk me into going pro. Caged fights."

"Caged fights," she repeated carefully.

"It keeps the combatants from throwing each other out of the ring, the way they do in wrestling." He sighed, embarrassed. "Wyatt tried to talk me out of it, but I wouldn't listen. I was going to be the most skilled MMA fighter ever born."

"But you gave it up after Bryan died."

"I had to. I'd lost it all. My enthusiasm for the sport, my confidence, a big bleeding part of my soul. Myself. I lost myself for a while." In truth, he still wasn't sure who or what he was now, but the longer he stood there with his arms around her, the more it seemed to come clear. "The point is," he told her, "I did a stupid thing, and I regret it. Most young men do at some point, and that's when they finally grow up. It just breaks my heart that Bryan won't have that chance."

"Oh, Ryder," she said, lifting her hands to his face. "I'm so sorry."

He shook his head. "No, no. Don't feel sorry for me. I'm standing here with the most beautiful woman in the world in my arms."

For the first time, he thought it might be possible to leave what had happened behind him, to have a full life, to find his place, his calling. That was reason enough to kiss her. But that wasn't why he did it.

He kissed her because she was the most wonderful thing he'd ever come across and he wanted all she was, all they could be.

Together.

Chapter Eleven

He didn't do it.

That thought kept popping into Jeri's consciousness. Ryder didn't kill her brother. Bryan had done it to himself. Bryan had caused his own death. What she didn't know was why that information had not been widely disseminated. Deciding to err on the side of caution, she called the private investigator and told him what she'd been told. He hemmed and hawed and finally said that he'd seen the autopsy report confirming that Bryan was using steroids, but Dena had sworn him to secrecy.

"Why would she do that?" Jeri demanded, but she already knew. Dena would do anything to punish Ryder, even if it meant using and lying to her own daughter.

The investigator hadn't seen the video of the sparring match, but he suspected that Dena had. "I know she took it to a technician. I gave her a name."

"And he told you that she'd had him edit the video?" Jeri pressed.

The investigator gusted a sigh into the telephone. "I didn't want to know. Okay?"

A shock of cold rattled through Jeri. Her mother had

tried to frame Ryder and use Jeri to spring the trap. The fact that Jeri had been handsomely paying an ethics-challenged private investigator to assist her mother's perfidy seemed surreal, but she could no longer deny the truth.

"You're fired," Jeri said, ending the call.

Sitting on the edge of her bed, she dropped her head into her hands and faced facts. She'd wanted to believe her mother's version of events. She'd wanted Ryder to be at fault. If he—or someone—wasn't at fault, then she had to accept that God had let this happen for reasons she might never know. It was so much easier to fix blame, to have someone to hate, to feel something other than sadness and grief. She'd helped her mother do this. She'd even whispered lies to reporters in Houston to keep the story alive, thinking she was buying time to get to the truth.

And when Ryder found out, she'd be as dead to him as Bryan, except Ryder wouldn't think as kindly of her as he did her brother.

Twisting onto her stomach, Jeri lay face down and sobbed, but she didn't have a lot of time to indulge her feelings. Ryder was waiting. She began to pray, and that calmed her. Thinking clearly again, she realized that she wanted to tell Ryder everything, but she didn't dare, not until she could convince him how much she cared for him. She needed time.

No matter what happened, she always seemed to need time, but she'd blown so much money on the investigator she couldn't afford to miss any more competitions. The only solution was to make the most of the time she had with Ryder.

After that kiss, she'd felt happy, ridiculously so, and

Ryder had seemed the same. But it wasn't real. He didn't know who she was, and she had to decide what she was going to do next. Her options were either to leave here at once or try to stake an emotional claim on the man she'd come here to ruin.

She knew what she wanted to do. She just didn't know if she had a right to or any chance of success. Still, what did she have to lose at this point?

"Okay, Lord," she whispered. "Here goes. I'll understand if it doesn't work out the way I hope."

Grimly determined, she dried her eyes, splashed cold water on her face and went out to meet him. Ryder was waiting beside her truck when she got downstairs. He smiled, and every instant of the kiss they'd shared swept through her. An overwhelming sense of relief swiftly followed.

Ryder didn't do it. He hadn't killed her brother.

That didn't mean he would forgive her lies and vicious intentions.

He opened the passenger door for her, and despite her fears, she couldn't keep back her smile. Running down the steps, she went straight to him. Laughing, he caught her in his arms and turned her into the open truck cab.

"Let's go get some horses, darlin'. We have work to do."

She popped up onto her toes to kiss him swiftly before hitching herself up into the passenger seat and handing him the keys. He laughed as he jogged around and got in on the driver's side.

They worked like a team, as if they'd been working together for years, hooking up the trailer, loading the horses, stowing her feed and gear. After they got her horses settled at Loco Man Ranch, they saddled

Gladiator, Star and Betty, and walked them out to the practice site. Then Jeri set up the timer, mounted and went to work.

Glad was eager and strong, driving the turns with his hind legs and laying out those long, effortless strides. The longer she ran him, the faster his times got. She traded him for Star only when his run times started to climb.

"Wow," Ryder exclaimed, lifting her down from the saddle. "That was amazing."

"Let's hope Star is as eager. I think they were happy to be back in the trailer, even for a short ride."

He'd already tightened Star's saddle, so she was ready to go. He threw Jeri up into the seat and began walking Glad, who didn't even bother with his usual balk. Ryder made sure to walk Glad by the timer at the end of every run and call out Star's numbers to Jeri. Star proved a little headstrong at first, but she soon calmed and got down to business. By the end, she was coming within a blink of Glad's time. Jeri ended the practice because she could feel Star tiring, but the horse just wouldn't pull back. Jeri feared the animal would hurt herself, run until she dropped from exhaustion.

Betty, on the other hand, couldn't seem to settle in to work, but Jeri kept at her until she finally began co-operating. After half a dozen good runs, Jeri called it a day. Then, feeling stiff, she went through her standing stretches while Ryder cooled down Betty. They led all three horses back to the stable, stowed the tack in her trailer and walked, arm in arm, to the house.

That became the pattern for the next two days. The evenings were spent watching television in the den, playing games with Tyler, who felt at loose ends after Frankie went home for the day with his parents, and on the last night, at prayer meeting, where Ryder requested prayers for her safe travel and success in the competition. Afterward, he gassed up the truck for her and helped her pack everything she needed.

Tack, hay and bedding for the horses crammed the truck bed, all securely protected from the weather, while feed and water filled the tanks and bins tucked into the trailer body. Several changes of clothing hung in the tiny cupboard that served as a closet in the sleeping compartment of the trailer. Other necessities filled the narrow drawers beneath it.

Living in a seven-foot-by-six-foot space required clever packing and making do with the barest comforts, but Jeri had done this for long enough to have it down to a science. Besides, she couldn't afford the roomier, more luxurious trailers, and this way she could be close to her horses at night. Not all rodeos provided top-notch security, after all, and her horses were very valuable.

Every evening ended the same, with her and Ryder standing outside her bedroom door, kissing good-night.

That last night, he leaned in and whispered, "I never thought I'd find you."

She whispered back, "I never thought I wouldn't want to leave you."

They parted with smiles, and when she crept out in the heavy darkness before dawn the next morning, he stood waiting for her again.

They loaded the horses in near silence.

All too soon, it was time to hit the road. She didn't want to go. Well, she did, just not alone.

He walked her to the driver's door. "Blow 'em away, darlin'. Blow 'em away."

"I wish you could come with me."

Smiling, he slid an arm around her waist and pulled her close. "Someday maybe."

She knew exactly what he meant. Someday they could travel together. If they were married. Oh, if only.

She removed her hat and wrapped her arms around his neck. He chuckled.

"Who'd have thought I'd crave the feel of your hat dangling between my shoulder blades?"

"Not me," she admitted. "Not in a million years." She went up on tiptoe and kissed him.

He drove her back down onto her heels, bending over her in a way that made her feel sheltered and safe. She knew suddenly that if she didn't go that very moment, she never would.

Tearing herself away, she got into the truck and started the engine. He stepped away, lifting his shoulders against the cold, and rammed his hands into his pockets. Ruthlessly, she yanked the transmission into gear and drove forward.

Her last sight of him was in the rearview mirror, standing in the glow of her taillights, watching her drive away from him.

She cried halfway to the Kansas state line and prayed the rest of the way.

It was the longest, most confusing weekend of his life.

At times, Ryder couldn't stop smiling. Then, all at once, fear would hit him.

What if she never returned?

He knew without doubt that she would come back if only for Dovie and Betty, but what if she couldn't? Accidents happened. He knew that all too well, so he compulsively checked the weather reports.

Those moments of fear appalled, confused and shamed him. He spent long hours talking to God about it and keeping away from his family, who always wanted to know if he'd spoken to her. He had not.

The urge to call her sometimes overwhelmed him, but he couldn't make himself do it. Too often Ryder had been casually involved with women who wanted more from the relationship than he could give them. Sometimes, just kissing a woman good-night at the end of a perfectly innocuous date could make her think he was interested in more. This time, he feared the reverse.

He feared that he was reading more into all that had passed between them than Jeri did. Besides, Jeri was working, busy. He could imagine how much she had to do all on her own, and he didn't want to bother or burden her. Or find out that some other guy more in tune with her world was out there tempting her.

Worry got its claws into him, and he couldn't seem to shake it. What if she changed her mind about him? She might talk it over with her friends, revealing all she knew, and be influenced by their disgust of him. Even without that, she might not be anywhere near as into him as he was into her.

And what if he called her and heard another man's voice in the background? Surprisingly, that thought plagued him more than any other. She owed him no fidelity, after all. Why, she could have a boyfriend in every town.

He didn't believe it.

He didn't want to believe it.

He reminded himself that he was the one she kissed, the one she went all soft and girly for, the one against whose chest she sighed and smiled and snuggled.

A beauty like her, though, could have any man she wanted. Maybe she didn't truly want him.

On Monday, he saw that a storm had dumped snow all along her route. He couldn't help thinking that he should be with her, keeping her safe. As if he could control the weather! The compulsion to express his concern got the better of him, so he texted her.

Watch the weather and take care on the roads.

After a few minutes, she texted back. Roads clear. Be home tonight.

Home.

That one word calmed his fears and restored balance to his mood. That didn't mean he wasn't anxious.

He was pacing the floor in the bunkhouse when headlights flashed across the window around 9 p.m. Grabbing his coat, he ran out without his hat. He reached for the handle on the truck door before she even brought the rig to a full stop.

She bailed out without a coat, grinning. He reached for her, and she threw her arms around him. His every fear faded away like so much mist in the wind.

"Welcome home, darlin'. How'd it go?"

She pulled back and reached inside for her jacket. "Second place. By eight hundredths of a second."

He whistled and helped her slip on the down coat. "You'll get 'em next time."

She laughed. "That's what everyone said. But, man, I've got work to do. I don't have to actually leave again until Friday, though."

"But you should, right?"

She made a face. "Right."

"Well," he said, "it's just Fort Worth. That's not too far away."

A thought had been germinating in the back of his mind. A certain friend had let Ryder know that he had moved from Houston to Dallas, and Dallas was just a hop, skip and jump away from Fort Worth.

He looped an arm around her as they walked back to pull out the trailer ramp. "Second place is still in the money, right?"

"It sure is, and it was a good payout. Fort Worth will be better."

"Especially when you win," he told her.

She laughed. "From your lips to God's ears."

"That's just how it's been going, darlin'. Exactly like that."

Suddenly stopping in her tracks, she kept her arm through his. Sheer momentum turned him to face her. She reached up, placing her bare hand on the side of his neck. Instantly his pulse leaped into double time. Tilting her head just so, she kissed him.

The part of Ryder's brain that could still work thought that kissing a woman in a cowboy hat warmed a man more than a fire. But then, this woman would always warm him, hat or no hat, kiss or no kiss.

Jeri was home.

For now, that was all that mattered.

Home.

To Jeri, this felt more like coming home than anything ever had. Tired to the bone but reluctant to leave Ryder just yet, she sat at the tiny bar, looked into the tiny kitchen of the cramped bunkhouse and ate soup she didn't even want because he'd had it simmering on the stovetop. This was what it would be like to come home to Ryder on a routine basis.

The only thing better, in her mind, would be if he could travel with her, but that could only happen under certain ideal circumstances, and she was afraid to even think about that. Right now, frankly, she was too tired to think at all.

She'd left before 6 a.m. to avoid Denver traffic at its worst and allow enough time for her to make a couple stops and care for the horses and still get home before bedtime. Barely.

"Everything go okay?" Ryder asked, watching a small pot of hot chocolate warming on the two-burner stove.

She nodded and shrugged. "The road conditions were more difficult in places than I'd hoped, but that was this morning. It got better quickly."

"I couldn't help worrying about you," he admitted.

She couldn't help smiling about that. "I know. But I'm fine."

Ryder's concern warmed her. His text had been simple and to the point, but it had pleased her, nevertheless. Not since her brother had died had anyone expressed concern for her safety.

All weekend she'd wondered if Ryder would call, and more than once she'd nearly called him, but as soon as she'd think of it, she'd have to be somewhere or do something else. Because she used to text her brother the results of every contest, she'd wanted to reach out to someone after the results were in. She wasn't sure how much Ryder knew about barrel racing, however, and he hadn't tried to call her, so she'd texted her mom instead.

Dena had replied with At least you didn't break your neck.

Dena had always considered barrel racing to be dangerous and foolish, but she'd stopped lecturing Jeri about it long ago. Bryan, on the other hand, could do no wrong—no matter how dangerous his pastimes. Whatever he'd tried, Dena had supported him.

If Bryan hadn't been such a loving brother, Jeri could have been quite jealous of him. How ironic was it that the man her mom blamed for Bryan's death was the one to offer her the most support now?

"You must be tired," Ryder said, sliding a steaming cup of cocoa to her.

"Very." She abandoned the soup and took up the chocolate, sipping experimentally. "Mmm. Delicious."

They chatted about what had gone on at the ranch while she was away. Tina was chafing at the bit to be off bedrest but obeying doctor's orders, and so far, so good. Jake was as busy as a beaver, with people bringing him their autos from miles around.

"I've been spending half of every day helping him and the rest of the time with the horses."

"Hope my two weren't an added burden."

"Naw. Looked like Dovie and Pearl were going to be archenemies for a while, but now they're like best friends. That's why they're next to each other in the barn."

"I saw the way Pearl hangs her head over into Dovie's stall and how they chuff each other."

He chuckled. "Lots of sniffing and snuffling going on over there. Is it like that at the rodeo?"

She shook her head. "Unless they know each other really well, we tend to keep our stock separated. Safer that way."

"I figured."

Jeri drained the cup and set it on the counter. "I'm going to fall asleep right here if I don't move."

"I'll walk you to the house."

"You don't have to do that."

"I want to."

Tired as she was, she wanted that, too, so she let him help her into her coat, waiting until he'd slipped on his and settled his hat into place. She linked arms with him, and they walked out into the cold, across the yard and through the carport to the house. He didn't stop there, though.

He walked her all the way up to her room. It was well after ten o'clock, and the household had retired, so they stayed silent, walking hand in hand. They came to a stop in front of her door. Before he had a chance to leave her, she looped her arms around his neck, her hat in her hand.

"There it is again," he whispered, smiling down at her. "Right where it belongs."

She knew he was talking about her hat resting between his shoulder blades. She closed her eyes as he kissed her, so very content, so much at peace. He didn't linger, knowing she was tired.

"See you in the morning."

"Good night."

A few minutes later, Jeri slid down beneath the covers of a bed that seemed entirely hers now, in a room that felt more like home than any other she'd ever known.

Lightly touching her lips, she closed her eyes and thought about that kiss.

He wanted her. No doubt about it. He wanted her *now*, but he wouldn't when he knew the truth. That was what she had to remember.

That was not, however, what she dreamed.

Chapter Twelve

Jeri slept in the next morning then rose to learn Ryder was at the shop with Jake. He'd left a message with Kathryn, saying he'd taken care of her horses, so Jeri shouldn't worry about that.

Tina had asked to see her, so after she'd eaten, Jeri went into the master bedroom. Tina's baby bump had become a baby mountain, and she grimaced with pain even as Jeri eased down into the rocking chair that Wyatt had brought in.

"Are you okay?"

Tina waved a hand. "It comes and goes, but it's not bad, just the occasional ripple. The doctor says all is well."

Jeri relaxed. "That's good. My only real experience with birth has to do with animals."

"Well, I'm just thankful humans don't gestate for eleven months," Tina quipped. "That's right, isn't it? Horses are pregnant for eleven months?"

Jeri nodded. "Thereabouts."

Tina put her head back, looking heavenward. "Okay,

God, I'm through complaining now. All I can say is, thank You for not making me a horse."

Laughing, Jeri said, "Most domestic livestock give birth in the spring. I want to be well settled before Dovie foals."

"That's your horse?"

"One of them."

"Everyone says Stark is excellent at delivering animals."

Jeri nodded. "I'm sure that's true. From my experience, I'd say he's a really good vet. All through high school I worked for a veterinarian. Can't count how many kittens, puppies, calves and foals I've helped deliver. Even a few sheep and a kid. That is, a goat."

Tina laughed. "Sounds like you're handy to have around."

"I don't know about that."

Elbowing her way higher in the bed, Tina grimaced again, but then she smoothed her hands over her swollen belly and smiled. "I wanted to tell you that you won't be our only guest for a few days. We have a couple coming in to visit their grandchildren. We'll be serving breakfast in the dining room for them in the morning, and it might get awkward if you eat with the family and they find out you're a guest."

Jeri felt a twinge of disappointment, hurt even. She'd started to feel like one of the family, which was ludicrous. Pasting on a smile, she nodded.

"No problem."

"Thank you. I knew you'd understand."

They talked about Denver for a few minutes, then Jeri went upstairs for her coat and got to work. She saddled Betty and rode her out to the practice field. They trained for nearly two hours before Jeri dismounted and walked the horse back to the barn. After currying the mare, she saddled Glad and rode him out to the field. When she looked up quite some time later, she found Ryder standing there watching, his forearms folded across the top pipe of the temporary fence section, a big grin on his face. Star waited in the small enclosure, saddled and ready. Jeri dismounted and walked Glad over to him.

"How long have you been there?"

"Not long enough. I do love to watch you work."

She laughed. "Guess I get pretty deep into it."

He nodded. "You talk to Tina?"

"Yes."

"You don't have to eat in the dining room if you don't want to."

She shrugged. "It's just breakfast. I can manage until I leave Thursday evening for Fort Worth."

He sighed. Then he smiled and reached for the reins. "I'd better take care of this old boy so he'll take care of you in Fort Worth."

She couldn't resist the impulse to peck a quick kiss on his lips before she turned over the reins. Then she watched him lead the horse away, wondering how many more times she'd be able to do that.

The fear that he'd discover exactly who she was and why she'd come there never left her. She could push it away while he was with her, but it was always there in the back of her consciousness. One day it was going to come crashing down around her.

And destroy her whole world.

The weather turned bitterly cold again on Tuesday night. Their new guests, a plump, gregarious couple who wore identical eyeglasses, joked that they'd brought the cold with them from Nebraska. The drop in temperature, however, didn't affect everyone so much as the wind, which built throughout the night until it howled with such ferocity that it woke Ryder from a sound sleep. Thankfully, no precipitation accompanied the gale, but with the temperature well below freezing, the wind drove cold into every crack and crevice.

Despite the constant hum of the central heating unit and a thermostat that told him the inside temperature hovered at sixty-eight degrees, Ryder huddled beneath his covers, feeling cold and isolated. Sleep seemed to blow away on the wind, which finally ebbed into silence some time before dawn. In the still, gray light, the grinding of a starter roused Ryder out of bed and into warm clothing. Shoulders hunched, he stepped out into a sharply cold, quiet morning. The sky was overcast with dirty gray clouds that hung so low they trapped sound at ground level. He even heard Jeri smack the steering wheel of her truck in frustration as he crossed the frozen yard.

He smiled. Somehow even her frustration pleased him. Trying not to chuckle at his own foolishness, he let himself into her truck on the passenger side.

"Trouble?"

"It won't start! Truck's got less than sixty thousand miles on it, and it won't start!"

He settled a gloved hand on the nape of her long, graceful neck. "Don't worry, darlin'. Most likely it's the battery. A cold snap will drain it. When Jake and Kathryn get here, he can take a look at it. Where are you off to so early anyhow?"

She shrugged, looking entirely too innocent. "Nowhere in particular. Thought I'd wander around town for a bit, maybe get some breakfast."

Ah. "You don't like the MacAfees?"

She sliced him with a glance. "It's not that. I—I don't even know the MacAfees. I just…" Tilting her head, she hid her face from him with the brim of her hat.

"You can have breakfast with the family if you prefer. In fact, I'll ask Kathryn to serve everyone in the dining room, if you like."

"No! I mean, being on the road, you…well, you get used to…privacy."

Privacy. Ryder thought it through. If he could name one thing Jeri seemed to have plenty of, it would be privacy. She traveled constantly. Alone. Normally, she worked long hours. Alone. While at Loco Man Ranch, she'd happily joined the family for meals day in and day out until now, so why the sudden need for privacy? He'd have thought the reverse would be true.

"So you don't want company?"

"I do," she answered quickly, but then her gaze shifted away again. "Some."

Some company.

He smiled. Not a cloud had moved, but the day felt brighter, lighter, warmer. *Him.* She meant him when she said she wanted "some" company.

Suddenly, he realized why the night had seemed so long and cold. The problem wasn't the temperature or even the wind. Sleep had eluded him because he'd missed her so keenly. He'd missed her desperately while she'd been away and had admitted it without reservation, if only to himself. For some reason, though, he'd missed her even more last night. He'd buried the feeling, but examined it now.

Just knowing she was there across the yard instead of with him, where he increasingly believed she should be, had kept him teetering on the knife-edge of restlessness. Nothing had felt right because she belonged with him. It was that simple.

Whether he deserved her or not, she belonged with him. He was never going to feel right again until she belonged *to* him. He was already hers. She just didn't know it yet.

"We can take my car into town."

Her head jerked around, and she beamed at him. "Okay."

Maybe some part of her did know that they were meant to be together, after all.

"You drive. That way I can lay back my seat and get comfortable."

Still beaming, she hopped out of the truck and ran around to the old sedan that had once belonged to Tina. He followed, marveling at how God had moved in his life, for this could be nothing else.

Maybe ten minutes later, while waiting to turn the sedan into a parking space in front of the diner, they met Jake, Kathryn and Frankie in Jake's truck. Right there in the middle of Main Street, Jake stopped and rolled down the window. Jeri did the same.

"What's up? Didn't expect to see the two of you in town this early. Especially not in that vehicle."

Ryder explained that they'd decided to hit the diner for coffee but that Jeri's truck wouldn't start so they'd come in the sedan.

"Uh-huh. 'Cause there's no coffee at the ranch." Grinning, Jake changed the subject. "Probably all that's wrong with the truck is the battery. I'll look at it after breakfast." He shook his head then, saying to Ryder, "You know you look ridiculous in that little car, right?"

Ryder rolled his eyes. "The fact is, I've been thinking about buying a truck of my own."

"Hoot Waller is selling that flashy, flame red Dodge Ram he bought a few months ago," Jake informed Ryder. "He wants everything checked out on it and says he'll make a good deal because it's got to go fast. Phyllis is divorcing him."

"They've only been married two or three years."

"Yep. Sad, isn't it?" With that, Jake rolled up his window and drove on.

"I don't understand it," Ryder commented, shaking his head. "Divorce just makes no sense to me."

"Sometimes it's the only way, though," Jeri said, turning into the parking space. "My mom had a friend whose husband drank too much and knocked her around. She tried every possible way to make it work. He'd stop drinking for a while, but then something would go wrong, he'd turn back to the bottle and then he'd take out his frustrations on her again. The last time, he stabbed her. She barely got out of the marriage alive."

"I don't understand that, either," Ryder said, frowning. "How does hurting someone make anything better? Especially someone smaller and weaker than you."

Killing the engine, Jeri sent him a pointed look. "Says the MMA fighter."

Ryder shook his head. "It wasn't about hurting anyone. Like boxing, it's a sport. You want to overpower your opponent, yes, but it's not about inflicting pain for some sense of satisfaction. It's about skill and technique, personal toughness and strength. There's a lot of posturing and showmanship, but I fought men who are good friends of mine, as well as some I didn't know well, and some I didn't like much, but I never wanted to hurt anyone. Yes, some fighters lose sight of MMA as a sport—mostly those who abuse drugs—but they don't last long. Outside the cage, I'd only fight to protect the innocent and those I love, and most of the fighters I know are the same way."

"Would you go back to cage fighting now?"

"No. Never again. And I wasn't the only one who dropped out after Bryan died."

Her gaze took on a faraway look. "I didn't know."

"No reason you should," he said, opening his car door.

She got out on her side and joined him on the sidewalk. They entered the little café to find Abe Tolly at the diner counter, hunched over a plate of flapjacks. He smiled broadly upon their entrance and turned on his stool. "Hey. One of my favorite young couples. I've been meaning to call you. Got a new listing you might be interested in."

Couple. Ryder watched Jeri, waiting to see if she would correct Tolly, but she just smiled and said, "We'll be glad to talk to you about it, but I'm not sure we'll have time to look at any properties this week. I've got to get ready for a competition in Fort Worth."

We.

Ryder lifted his hand to the small of her back in a purely possessive gesture and let himself brag. "She finished second in Denver last weekend, and she's determined to nail first place in Fort Worth."

"Good for you!" Tolly told her. "Property's not even

listed yet. You go get 'em in Fort Worth, and we'll talk about spending your winnings when you get back."

Jeri laughed. "Sure thing, Mr. Tolly. Thanks."

They ate breakfast in a booth in the far corner, lingering over coffee and talking quietly about the Fort Worth rodeo. Afterward, they went back to the ranch and took care of the horses. Ryder jump-started Jeri's truck before driving it over to Jake's shop, where Jake was eager to show Hoot Waller's truck to Ryder. It had all the bells and whistles, and the price was right, so Ryder took it out for a spin.

He drove first. Then Jeri got behind the wheel.

"It'll tow a trailer full of horses, no doubt about it. Comfortable, too."

He silently prayed about it all the way back to the shop.

Is this it, Lord? My girl? My truck? My future? Is this You telling me to go for it?

He thought again of Fort Worth. And Dallas. He thought, too, of a more substantial future. Paying cash for the truck wouldn't leave him with much savings or build his credit.

"Guess I better go to the bank."

Jake was glad to hear it. Clapping Ryder on the shoulder, he said, "We've taken care of you. Now, let's look at Jeri's truck."

Even after a jump start and driving the truck over to the shop, the engine wouldn't turn over. The battery was shot.

"I'll replace it with a heavy-duty model, wholesale. Might as well check out everything else. When did you last have the oil changed?"

Jeri grimaced. "I don't recall. I'm not very good at that sort of thing."

Ryder blinked at Jeri then looked to Jake. "The woman drives all over the country by herself, and she doesn't remember when she last had her truck serviced. Yow."

Jake grinned at Jeri and drawled, "Not that he worries about you or anything. We'll take care of it."

Jeri slid her hand into Ryder's. "Thank you."

"No problem," Jake told her, grinning, then he jerked his head at Ryder. "Take my truck back to the house. I'll drive Jeri's over when I'm done."

"Now that's service," Jeri said as Ryder walked her out to Jake's truck. "I absolutely love the way he's decorated the place."

"That's not Jake's doing. He can thank Kathryn for that."

"You should get her to decorate the bunkhouse for you."

"What? You don't like my gym motif?"

They both laughed.

As soon as they returned to the house, they got to work with the horses. Jake returned to the house for lunch, leaving her truck in the carport. Ryder and Jeri dragged in last. Ryder was shivering with cold, so he knew Jeri had to be frozen to the bone. Thankfully, Kathryn had a hot lunch ready. Afterward, Jeri said she was going to wait a couple of hours before getting back to work, to which Wyatt remarked, "You really need an indoor area to work in."

"Someday," she told him, rising to help clean up.

Someday, Ryder thought, he was going to build that covered arena for her. First things first, though.

He excused himself to take care of personal business. Deciding to go around Jake, he got on the phone with Hoot Waller and dickered his way down to an excellent purchase price for the truck before arranging to meet Hoot at the bank. He paved the way with a phone call to the loan officer there who handled the Loco Man line of credit. With a sizable down payment, the bank was only too happy to lend Ryder enough money to complete the purchase of the truck. With that done, he called his buddy in Dallas. Once the arrangements were made, he began praying again: first, that Jeri was coming to the same conclusions as he was; second, that he could keep his mouth shut; and third, that Jeri liked surprises.

They went to prayer meeting as usual, except that this time they drove Ryder's new truck, just the two of them, Ryder and Jeri. Ryder again requested prayer for her safety and success. Jeri prayed for guidance and some way to make Ryder forgive her secrets.

For the first time, she dreaded hitting the road, even for so short a drive. Despite the delight of being with Ryder again, she felt a deep, edgy sense of time running out. Still, she had to compete. She had to keep the money coming in, especially if she was actually going to find a place of her own, hopefully near Ryder.

Please, God, let it be near Ryder. Let him want me nearby.

He seemed to. Now. Everyone else seemed to take it for granted that they were together for good. Even the family treated them like a permanent couple, but how would they feel about her once they knew the truth?

Thursday came all too soon. Thankfully, the cold snap waned and warmer temperatures returned. Ryder helped her work the horses that morning. Then they packed the trailer. This was no ordinary rodeo, so twice the gear had to be packed, and that took twice the time. It was 7 p.m. before Jeri was ready to leave. She did not want to go, and she didn't know when she would return.

"I have to sign in and draw before I'll know when the first run will be. Then, if I don't make the finals—"

"You'll make them. You're going to win this one, remember?"

She smiled at Ryder's enthusiasm and confidence. "If I don't make the finals, I'll be back next week."

He shook his head. "As much as I want you home safe, it's not going to be next week."

"If I have a chance to finish in the money, I'll be there until after my last run. That could be a week from Sunday, maybe Saturday."

"I understand. You'll let me know, won't you? I can always check the standings on the computer, but I'd like to know before you race so I can pray for you."

"I'll let you know," she promised, a lump growing in her throat.

He hugged her, then kissed her, then handed her into the truck. "Let me know when you get there, too. Please."

"Yes. Absolutely."

After one more quick kiss, he stepped back and closed the door. Driving away after that was one of the toughest things Jeri had ever done. She could barely see through the tears that started to fall as soon as she turned onto the highway. Thankfully, the ride was relatively short. Less than four hours after leaving him, she called to tell him that she was checked in at the fair grounds and was about to set up camp in an off-site lot.

He kept her talking for a while, asking for details about where she was situated and if the site was safe. The area couldn't have been much safer. Constructed especially for those with personal mounts, the lot was fenced in, with sheltered animal pens all around the perimeter. The gates were closed at midnight, and visitors had to sign in and out. Campers were assigned spaces according to the sizes of their rigs and the number of animals they'd brought with them. Jeri had even been placed among other barrel racers, so she knew nearly everyone around her.

After they got off the phone, she unloaded the horses and bedded them down in their assigned shelter. Then she hooked her trailer up to the electricity and the sewer before changing into her warmest pajamas and crawling into her sleeping bag. Her narrow bed atop a long, rectangular storage locker—hence the name "coffin bed"—had never felt so lonely. She considered calling Ryder again, but he was probably long asleep at this point. She could wait until she knew when she would ride.

That happened the next morning. As soon as she saw which slot she'd drawn, she dialed up Ryder.

"First run is Saturday night. That's good. It gives me time to work the horses in this environment. Helps them settle. If I blow it, I'll be home Wednesday."

"You'll make the cut," he said matter-of-factly. "I know you will."

"If I do," she went on around a smile, "I'll have to stay around until at least next Saturday."

"But you won't find out if you win or not until Sunday. Right?"

"That's right. I'll be ready to hit the road the minute after I hear. Or I could come on in Saturday and let them notify me later. That is, *if* I win."

"You need to be there when the results come in," he insisted.

"I'll be home awfully late if I wait for the results."

"Just be ready to pick up that check and all the swag that goes with it. Don't worry about how late it might be. You'll be safe. I promise."

Her heart suddenly felt too big for her chest, and she wanted to say so much in reply to that. But she didn't dare. Not yet.

"I know. I always am. It's just…" Thinking quickly, she came up with, "There's more downtime here than usual."

In big rodeos like this that covered more than one weekend, some competitors hired others to deliver their horses then flew in and out when they were scheduled to compete. Jeri couldn't bring herself to turn her horses over to anyone else, though.

"I hear there's plenty to do," Ryder said, "a carnival midway, all sorts of exhibits and events."

"That's true. One of the local radio stations even sponsors dances."

"Well, there you go."

"Yeah, I guess." She didn't say that she wouldn't be attending any of those dances, not this year. She just couldn't imagine being with any other man now, even for a casual dance.

Deep in her heart, she knew that at some point Ryder would step out of her life, and she'd have to find a way to live without him. That shouldn't have seemed so daunting. She'd lived twenty-three years without Ryder

Smith, after all. Why, suddenly, did he now seem so essential to her well-being?

All she knew was that losing him was going to tear her apart. She couldn't even think about it. So she didn't. Instead, she pretended that all was well.

They were just a normal couple getting to know one another.

And falling in love.

God help her.

Chapter Thirteen

He drove down to Dallas on Friday afternoon, ate an early dinner with his buddy, and then informed said buddy that they were going to the rodeo. Oscar, nick-named Ox, didn't argue.

"Yeah, boy! We'll probably have to take the cheap seats, but let's go."

Ox chattered, mostly about his job, while Ryder navigated rush-hour traffic in the Dallas–Fort Worth Metroplex, those years of doing battle with Houston drivers paying off. Ryder had pulled up the route on his truck's in-dash GPS screen, so he didn't even have to use his cell phone for directions. The drive was almost sixty-five miles, and the dashboard clock read twelve minutes past eight o'clock when he parked. They were just outside the fence surrounding a yard full of trucks and trailers lined by animal shelters. Ox twisted in his seat and stared at him.

"Okay, what gives?"

Ryder just shook his head and got out. At the gate-house, he asked where he could find number sixty-seven. The guy pointed to a far corner. Ryder set off,

Ox on his heels. As they wound through the mishmash of rigs, Ryder pulled out his phone and dialed. Jeri answered at once.

"Ryder?"

"Hey, darlin'. What're you doing?"

"A girl," Ox said under his breath. "Well, it's about time."

Ryder glared at him, but Ox just grinned.

"Nothing much," Jeri said to Ryder. "Just relaxing in my trailer with my friend Lacy before I have to start warming up Star."

"So Star's first up then, huh?"

"Yes."

He heard a female voice in the background, asking, "Who is that?"

Jeri must have covered the microphone, for her reply was muffled, but he had no trouble understanding her when she said, "My boyfriend."

Boyfriend. He wanted to crow, but he just kept talking and walking. "Got some time for company?" When he spotted her rig, he picked up his pace.

"Company?"

"Uh-huh. Didn't I tell you that my friend Ox lives in Dallas?" He came to a halt in front of the sleeping compartment of her trailer.

"Ox? No. No, I'd remember that. Is he here? In Fort Worth, I mean."

"He is." With that, Ryder reached out and knocked on her door. "So am I."

She dropped the phone. Someone was squealing like a stuck pig, but Jeri didn't have time to realize that it was her. She was too busy trying to get the door opened. Finally, it gave way, and there he stood, her every hope embodied in one dear man. She leaped at him. She could no more stop herself from throwing her arms around his neck than she could have stopped the earth from turning.

"Ryder! You're here!"

Laughing, he caught her against him, her feet dangling off the ground. She was glad that she'd worn the long-sleeved turquoise top. In her skinny brown jeans and turquoise-inlaid boots, her hair plaited loosely, she knew she was looking her best.

"Got the wheels, got a place to stay." Without ever taking his eyes off her, he waggled a thumb at the tall, slender cowboy next to him. "Why wouldn't I come see my girl run?"

My girl. Overjoyed, she kissed the smile on his face. Finally, he lowered her to her feet. Then he made the introductions.

"This here is Oscar. Ox, this Jeri—"

"Bogman," Oscar finished for him. Then he took off his droopy black felt hat and beat Ryder across the shoulders with it. "You dog! You didn't let on at all, and here you are with none other than Jeri Bogman kissing your ugly face."

Ryder could not have grinned any wider. "You wouldn't have believed me if I'd told you."

"No way." Ox rolled the brim of his felt hat in his hands and nodded at Jeri. "He don't even follow rodeo like I do."

"He does now," Ryder declared.

"Well, he may not know rodeo, but he sure knows horses," Jeri said, leaning into Ryder and smiling up at him.

Here. He was here. For her. She could hardly believe it.

Lacy stuck her head out the door then. Dressed in black jeans and a ruby-red shirt, her black hat turning her blond hair into liquid gold, she looked Ryder up and down, raised her eyebrows then did the same to Ox, who looked thunderstruck. Jeri giggled.

"Guys, this is Lacy Maddox. Lacy, Ryder and Ox."

"Well, now, this is propitious," Ox announced, hanging his thumbs in the waistband of his jeans. "Maddox. Ox. Sounds like fate to me."

Lacy leaned a slender hip against the frame of the open door and folded her arms, staring at Ox, who wasn't a bad-looking fellow, if you liked long and stringy. She apparently did, for she smiled at Jeri and said, "Girl, you sure can pick 'em."

"And how," Jeri agreed.

Ryder folded her close then and kissed her like he meant it, right there in front of God and everyone. Jeri had never been so happy, and for once—just for a while—she refused to be afraid about what the future might hold.

When he lifted his head, she smiled up into his handsome face, and said, "I'm so glad you're here."

"Ah, darlin'," he said with a lopsided grin, "I don't want to be anywhere else."

Lacy shoved the brown felt hat at Jeri then. "You'd better get on the move, cowgirl."

Just then the preset alarm on Jeri's phone went off inside the trailer. Tearing herself away from Ryder, she rushed inside to find it. She turned off the alarm, then took the hat Lacy still held and settled it onto her head. Thinking quickly, Jeri began issuing requests.

"Lacy, can you snag a couple of passes for the guys?"

"I'll head over there right now." The tall blonde stepped down out of the door.

"Better take Ox with you," Jeri called, deciding to change her belt and put on a prize buckle. "I need Ryder to see to Star."

He leaned into the trailer. "Just tell me what to do."

"She's saddled, so just let her out. We'll walk her over to the fairgrounds. I'll be right there."

"On it." He disappeared.

Jeri stripped off her belt, quickly threaded another through the loops and fastened it before throwing on a hip-length, dark brown, fringed leather coat. Then she paused to look at herself in the mirror. She saw in her own face what everyone else must see. She saw love.

She loved that man, and she was going to make this time with him count. If nothing else, she'd have sweet memories to comfort her in the dark days. Meanwhile, she'd have him. For a while, she'd have him.

Coming here had been the right thing to do, Ryder decided. No spectator seats for him and Ox. They had passes that let them into the warrens of pens and chutes hidden from the crowd flanking the arena. After they warmed up, he walked Star, with Jeri on board, back to the end of the long aisle where they'd start their run. Jeri shrugged out of her jacket and handed it to him. With so many penned animals around and wranglers rushing here and there, the temperature was as comfortable in the back area as in the enclosed arena.

Star could barely contain her energy. A speaker blared the smooth baritone of the announcer, and as soon as he said Jeri's name, she heeled the horse.

Ryder had never seen Star hit it like that, head down, tail high, hooves a blur. *Ride with her, Lord*, he prayed silently. Running after them, he made it to the end of the aisle as they pulled away from the first barrel and raced for the second.

"Go, baby, go," he muttered, gripping her coat, as they rounded that barrel and flew toward the third. Suddenly, they were pulling back onto the straight. "Bring her home now. Bring her home!"

He didn't realize he was shouting until he stopped to flatten himself against the rough wood wall as Jeri flew by. Star seemed to pick up speed the longer she ran. Jeri started reining in the mare about halfway down the aisle, but it was obvious that Star wanted to run and run some more. Demonstrating that with a kick of her heels and the pluming of her tail, she strained against the bit, prancing as if to say, "I did it! Let's do it again!" Jeri was laughing when Ryder reached them.

"'If I make the finals,'" he teased, repeating her words back to her as he led Star out of the way. The next racer was already lined up. "Darlin', you just set the bar for your competitors up in the stratosphere."

"I didn't hear the time. Did you?"

He told her what the announcer had called, surprised he'd heard and remembered the numbers. Jeri pumped a fist as Ox and Lacy rushed up to them.

"You're killing us, Jeri," Lacy complained, but she was smiling. "That was a run for the record books. Congratulations."

"You'll beat my time, see if you don't."

"I'll be happy if I wind up just in the general area," Lacy proclaimed.

"This needs celebrating," Ox insisted.

Ryder smiled up at Jeri. "Maybe we'll make that dance tonight."

She beamed and stayed in the saddle as Ryder handed her coat up to her and took Star's reins into his hands. He walked the mare to cool her down before heading back out into the cold. After they reached the shelter, he and Jeri worked together to unsaddle and curry the animal.

"When does Lacy ride?" he asked.

"Tomorrow night."

"And when do you ride next?"

"Tuesday. Then, if nothing goes wrong, Friday. But I'm giving clinics on Wednesday and Thursday. That way, I get arena time to practice."

"What can I do to help? I don't know if I should leave early enough to avoid the rush-hour traffic or wait until it's calmed down."

She goggled at him. "You're going to stay for the whole rodeo?"

"Planned on it." The smile that kept overtaking him got him again. "Thought I'd follow you home after it's all said and done."

She stared at him for several long seconds, her eyes growing brighter and brighter as tears gathered in them. He lifted a hand to skim the line of her jaw.

"Sweetheart? Something wrong? I—I don't have to stay. It was rash of me to think—"

Abruptly, she kissed him. "You've never done a rash, presumptuous, thoughtless thing in your life, Ryder Smith. Don't you think I know that? Don't you know how much it means to me that you chose to be here? And if you think I don't want you here, you're nuts."

"That has been said."

"Not by me." Grasping him by the sleeves, she shook him, as much as it was possible to shake a human mountain. "Listen. From now on, avoid rush-hour traffic. It's safer that way. I just wish you were staying here in Fort Worth."

"Let's just be glad Ox decided to take a transfer to Dallas when his company offered it."

"Oh, I am. I'm beyond thankful. Remind me to tell him so."

"I'll tell him for you," Ryder chortled, only half teasing.

Smiling brightly, she grabbed his hand, and they all but ran back to where Ox and Lacy waited.

They danced all the slow dances that night. Ryder was exhausted by the time he flopped down on Ox's couch to sleep, but he met Jeri for lunch the next day then helped her exercise the horses, and that night the four of them hit the carnival. It was every bit as cold in Fort Worth as in War Bonnet, but Ryder didn't feel it. With his arm locked around Jeri, he felt as warm as if he was in front of a toasty fire.

They weren't allowed fires at the place where she was camped, so on Sunday evening, after attending the Cowboy Church service provided for the contestants and exhibitors, the four of them gathered at Ox's apartment. Forgoing the rodeo entirely that night, they ate steaks carried in from a local restaurant in front of the tiny fireplace tucked into the corner of the living room. They laughed and talked late into the night. Then Ryder walked Jeri downstairs to kiss her goodbye beside Lacy's brother's truck. A bronc rider, he traveled with Lacy, but thus far they'd seen nothing of him.

After Lacy came down and the women left, Ryder

climbed the stairs to Ox's apartment again. His friend grinned like the proverbial Cheshire cat, so Ryder knew he was in for a ribbing. Deciding to beat Ox to the punch, he plopped down on the sofa and popped off.

"So, you got Lacy under your spell yet?"

To his surprise, Ox sobered. "Doubt it. A woman like that is plumb outta my league, Ry. I drive heavy equipment for a living."

"Nothing wrong with that. I can't even say that much. I'm hoping to raise horses, but right now I'm just a glorified ranch hand. And look who I'm with."

Ox lifted his feet to the battered coffee table, stacking one booted ankle atop another. "Ain't that the truth! No offense, friend—you know I love you like a brother—but it just don't figure. She's not as famous as some, but she will be. You know that, don't you?"

"I know it," Ryder confirmed. "I know it in my bones."

"I mean, look at her. Either of them. They're gorgeous."

"I see her in my dreams, Ox."

Oscar shook his head. "If you'd stuck with the cage fighting, you might've been somebody someday, too, but you gave that up."

"You know why," Ryder put in quietly.

"She know about that?"

Ryder nodded. "She does. That's part of it. I never imagined a woman who could trust me after Bryan's death."

"Dude. How many times we gotta go over that? You're—"

"Not to blame." Ryder finished for him, holding up hand, flat palm facing his friend. "I know. I know.

But knowing it and feeling it are two different things."
Looking down, he tugged off his boots. "I'm getting
there, though."

"Because of her?" Ox probed.

Ryder shrugged, unwilling to reveal more than he
had. "Let's just say, I'm in a good place right now."

"That's my point exactly. Against all odds, Jeri Bogman seems fall-down-blind, slap-me-silly crazy about
you. Grab her while you can and hold on tight. Before
it's too late."

Ryder smiled. "What do you think I'm doing here?"

"Well, you didn't come just to see me."

"I'd have gotten around to it," Ryder insisted.

Grinning, Ox threaded his fingers over his belt
buckle. "I don't care why you came. I'm just glad you're
here. And if it keeps throwing that luscious blonde my
way, *I'll* kiss you at your wedding."

Laughing, Ryder held up his thumb and forefinger,
showing a small gap between them. "Getting just a tad
ahead of yourself, don't you think?"

"Not much," Oscar said. "Not if you're as smart as
I think you are. Act fast. Before this thing blows up in
your face."

And breaks my heart, Ryder thought.

"She won," Ryder announced on Monday, hanging
up their coats in the kitchen at the Loco Man ranch
house.

They'd delayed their departure from Fort Worth until
after rush hour that morning, so Jeri was surprised to
find the family still at lunch. Even now, she could hardly
believe that she'd taken the top spot in Fort Worth. Her
time that first night had been the best overall, but the

later runs had been fast enough to keep anyone else from catching her. The aggregate time had come in at sixteen and four-tenths of a second, not a record but the best of the ten-day event.

Wyatt wiped his mouth with a napkin and got up to come toward them. "Winning at a Fort Worth rodeo is big stuff. Congratulations, Jeri." He lightly embraced her then pulled in Ryder for a backslapping bear hug. "We missed you."

"Boy, did we ever," Jake said. "I've spent so much time tending horses, I'm starting to look like one."

"You had that problem before I left," Ryder shot back, grinning.

Kathryn snickered behind her hand. "What Jake really means is that he hasn't had as much time to tinker with that old Jeep as he wants."

Chuckling and shaking a finger at Jake, Wyatt walked back to the table. "You better watch it or Delgado will dicker you out of that thing. He wants it bad."

"Aw, I'll probably let him take it and drive it when I'm done. We'll title and tag it to the ranch and let him use it. We sure use his old truck enough."

"Now we have another," Ryder said, escorting Jeri to the table.

She'd gotten so used to waiting for him that she hadn't even thought of walking to the table on her own.

"What?" Wyatt scoffed, teasing. "That rodeo truck you bought? Why, that's just for show, isn't it?"

"It got quite a lot of notice this past week," Jeri said, joining in the fun. "As did its owner. I had to warn off more cowgirls than I could count."

"What?" Ryder squawked, pulling out her chair.

Jeri grinned. "Everyone kept asking where I found

my new wrangler. I had to tell them you're the last of
your kind. Besides, not many can handle the likes of
you."

"Or would," Jake added dryly.

Everyone laughed. Ryder ran a hand through his
rumpled hair, smiling sheepishly. He took his place at
the table next to Jeri, who filled her plate then his, making sure he got the lion's share. It was good to be home.
How easy it was to think of this place as part hers now.
She had to forcibly remind herself that it was not.

"How's Tina?"

"Restless but otherwise well. She'll want a detailed
rundown on your week."

"I'll go in and visit her after I eat."

Wyatt asked about Oscar. Ryder, who seemed
strangely pensive, lifted his head and answered.

"Ox is good. He'd rather be living in Fort Worth than
Dallas, but the job is just up the road from his apartment, so I imagine he'll stay put for now. It was good
to see him."

"He's a card," Jeri added. "Kept my friend Lacy in
stitches."

Jeri wished she'd see Lacy over the coming weekend.
So many of the single women involved in rodeo were
party girls, but that wasn't Jeri's style. Of like mind,
Lacy was always a welcome sight. Unfortunately, they
were headed in opposite directions for at least the next
couple of weeks. Maybe if Lacy were coming to the
competition in Montana, Jeri wouldn't miss Ryder so
much. Leaving him this time was going to be excruci-
ating, but they'd settled that back in Fort Worth.

"It just isn't wise, darlin'," he'd said, sitting on the
fender of her trailer with his arm looped about her. He

wouldn't even step foot inside the tiny cabin. "Staying with a friend sixty-some miles away and checking into a motel room on my own are two different levels. I'd love to be there to support you, but it would be just too expensive. Still, you know my heart'll be right there with you, every step of the way."

She'd buried her face in the curve of his neck, feeling such love for this man that she could barely think of anything else. If only her mother hadn't become more and more strident over the past week. Several times Jeri had walked away from Ryder and their friends to take her mom's angry calls. Finally, Jeri had just stopped answering the phone. Dena was furious that Jeri had fired the investigator and flatly refused to answer any of Jeri's questions concerning Bryan. Instead, she continuously demanded that Jeri find some way to incriminate Ryder, and even the feeblest defense of him had resulted in a cataclysm of threats.

"Nice? He's a nice man? How nice was he when he was breaking your brother's neck? If you blow this, you're no daughter of mine, Jeri Jane Bogman! Do you hear me? You'll be a disgrace to your brother's memory, and as dead to me as he is!"

Jeri trembled every time she remembered the ugly words, but all she could do was pray for God to hand her a solution. Her mother was wrong about Ryder, but Jeri feared that nothing anyone could say would change Dena's mind.

It was a short week. Because the drive to Montana meant nearly twenty-four hours on the road, she had to leave early on Wednesday. Nevertheless, she and Ryder made time to look at properties with Abe Tolly, discussing the pros and cons of each as if they might buy it.

"That hilltop over there is a good spot for a house," Ryder pointed out at the last place.

Jeri's heart soared even as her stomach turned over. "You mean, build a house?"

"Wouldn't have to be anything fancy."

She pretended she didn't understand what he was suggesting. "You should see what I'm living in now. Not that I'm there much. The house is practically falling down. I don't know why I even pay the rent."

He turned in a circle then, gazing at the landscape around them. "Seems odd to be talking about buying property when the Loco Man has so much space to spare."

She tried for a chuckle, but it came out more of a stuttering sigh. "Your brothers aren't going to sell me a piece of Loco Man, not even a measly hundred and sixty acres."

"No," he agreed quietly, "but they'd give it to me." Stepping closer, he spoke in a near whisper, his voice a deep, rumbling caress. "I know it's too soon for this, but—"

Grasping him by the waist, she pressed against him, hiding her face in the hollow of his shoulder. "Don't say it. Not yet. I keep thinking you'll change your mind, that I'll wake up one morning and you'll look at me like you don't even know me. And you don't. Not really."

He slid his hand under the heavy curtain of her hair and cupped the nape of her neck. "I know I won't ever feel like this about anyone else. Girl, I'm head over heels in—"

She put her hand over his mouth. "Please. How am I supposed to leave you once you've said that? I can barely stand it now. And I must go. I must."

He smiled against her fingertips then tugged her hand away. "You're right. Your career has to come first. It's not like the land is going to get up and walk off. Let's put Montana behind us and plan for February. Valentine's Day is coming up."

"Your birthday's first," she reminded him.

He grinned. "How do you know when my birthday is?"

"I found out, okay?"

"Okay."

"And I'll be here. I promise."

"Darlin', that's a Sunday," he pointed out. "You'd have to leave the rodeo early to make it back here by Sunday."

She made a face. "I want to be here for your birthday."

"I know. Maybe next year."

But would next year come for the two of them? If only she knew how to fix this mess. Why hadn't she come straight at him and demanded the truth from the very beginning? But no, she'd had to lie, pretend she knew nothing of his history with her own brother.

"You going to tell me when your birthday is?" Ryder asked, smiling.

"July. The eighth."

He rubbed his hands together. "Ooh. That gives me a good long time to plan."

"Now, you behave yourself, Ryder Smith," she ordered teasingly. "At this point, I wouldn't put anything past you."

"Well, no, honey. You shouldn't," he retorted, winking at her.

She laughed. She couldn't help herself. Despite the

doom that seemed to hang over her, it was impossible not to be happy around him. Clasping her hand, he turned to the Realtor, who had maintained a respectful distance. "Abe, we need to get back to the ranch. Jeri's headed to Montana shortly, and there's lots to do."

The dignified old cowboy nodded, a secretive smile on his weathered face. Jeri had no idea what he might be thinking.

But it couldn't be what she was thinking. That she was a walking, smiling lie.

Chapter Fourteen

She made her run on Friday night and was disqualified for knocking over not one but two barrels. Furious with herself, she vowed that she'd make no more short turn-around trips. If she'd been working from Texas, she'd have driven straight to Montana after Fort Worth, giving herself time to make a leisurely transition and rest before competing.

Remembering those few days at Loco Man Ranch with Ryder and the rest of the family, she asked herself if the stopover had been worth it. Homesickness swamped her with an intensity that reduced her to hot tears. Suddenly the stupidity and uselessness of it all hit her like a Mack truck.

What was the point of driving halfway across the country to compete when Ryder waited for her back in Oklahoma? What difference did it make if she won or lost? If he wasn't with her, nothing else mattered—not the standings, not the money, not even the horses.

Determined to make it back to the ranch in time for his birthday, she loaded up and headed out before dawn the next morning, pouring coffee down her throat to stay awake, a sense of urgency spurring her. Driving straight through, she made it—barely. The hour was nearing 11 p.m. when she pulled into the Loco Man compound on Sunday evening. She didn't expect Ryder to be waiting because she hadn't informed him that she was coming. Instead, she'd thought to surprise him and keep him from worrying about her into the bargain.

She almost wept when she saw that the lights were still on in the house. That didn't mean Ryder was in there, but it might mean he was still awake. Tired, anxious and desperate to see him, she grabbed the small, wrapped package off the seat next to her, left the horses standing in the trailer and ran for the house, forgetting her coat. After Montana, Oklahoma didn't even feel cold to her.

The instant she opened the door, she knew something bad had happened. Only Wyatt looked at her. Sitting with his back to the door, Ryder merely bowed his head. Jake deliberately looked away. Her heart *thunking* and stomach twisting, she advanced into the room, mentally grabbing at every conceivable problem or tragedy. The most urgent possibility had her stumbling to a halt.

"Tina? Has something happened to Tina?"

"Tina's fine," Wyatt stated, his voice flat and hard. "As fine as she can be, anyhow."

But something was wrong. Jeri could feel it. "Then what's happened?"

"Nothing much," Jake snapped, glaring at her. "Just character assassination, half-truths and outright lies. You know, business as usual with you, Miss Bogman. It is Bogman, isn't it? Not Averrett."

They knew.

The world seemed to tilt, crack and splinter, the pieces falling away to leave the same tableau before her: Ryder bowed and silent, Wyatt grim and hard, Jake furious. Somehow, though, the scene had been transported to an entirely different plane of existence, one where every warm light, every welcoming smile, all sweetness and hope had been banished. She had to stiffen her knees to stay upright.

"I can explain."

"Explain this," Wyatt said, rising to toss a folded newspaper at her feet.

Crouching, Jeri laid aside the gift-wrapped package and reached for the paper, carefully unfolding it. There on the front page of Friday's edition of the *Tri-County Weekly* was a publicity photo of Ryder from his cage-fighting days, bare-chested and looking fierce. The headline read, "Local Resident Accused of Murder." Crying out, she went to her knees, quickly scanning the print with tear-filled eyes.

It was all there, anonymously sourced, even the fact that he had been cleared by Houston authorities. That snippet of information had been buried in a deluge of suspicions and accusations that sounded so incredibly familiar that she knew they could only have come from her mother, whose name was not mentioned. Jeri's was, though. She read the sentence silently, while her heart cried out in anguish.

"Jeri Bogman, the victim's half sister and well-known barrel racer, has personally been investigating what many consider to be a grave miscarriage of justice."

"I didn't do this," she managed, her voice trembling as tears spattered the page. "I would never—"

Ryder's chair suddenly screeched across the floor. Before she could make it to her feet, he strode past her and out the door, crushing beneath his booted foot the package containing the gift she'd had made for him.

She clapped a hand over her mouth, trapping the scream building in her throat. Gulping, she struggled to her feet and turned an imploring gaze on his brothers.

"I would never do this to him. I love him."

"Right," Jake snarled. "You love the man who killed your brother." He stabbed a forefinger at the paper. "*Murdered* him, it says in there."

"It was an accident," she squeaked.

"But you coming here wasn't," Jake accused.

That she couldn't deny. "No." She shook her head.

Wyatt tossed another paper at her. "At least the Sunday edition of the Ardmore paper was more circumspect." He tossed another. "It only got three inches of space in Oklahoma City. I guess that's something to be thankful for."

Jeri moaned, swaying. "I'm sorry. I'm so sorry. I never meant… when I came here, I only wanted the truth."

"Yeah," Jake said in a sarcastic tone. "The truth would be nice. Once in a while."

Wincing, Jeri couldn't think what else to say. She deserved everything he'd said and more. She had lied. She'd come here under false pretenses. And she'd fallen in love. For all the good that did anyone now.

"I think you should leave," Wyatt said in a quiet, level tone that brooked no argument.

For a long, tense moment, she couldn't make herself move. Then suddenly she couldn't bear to stay.

Blindly, Jeri turned and stumbled out of there, sobbing as the door closed behind her. She climbed back into her rig and drove away, leaving everything else behind her.

It hurt to breathe, so Ryder held his breath, but that hurt, too, so he gasped in air, rolled over in bed and stared at the ceiling, feeling like one big blob of pain. Losing Jeri was worse than anything he'd ever experienced, worse even than her lies. He'd been so young when his mom had died that he hadn't truly understood the ramifications. His father's death had come with a sense of relief. Al Smith's grief over his wife's passing had never diminished, and while the ravages of his cancer had been horrific, the ordeal was short-lived and had ended with a sense that he'd found peace at last. Bryan's death had been much worse, but even that paled in comparison to this. Try as he might and despite an overwhelming sense of betrayal, Ryder simply couldn't stop loving or missing her. He was his father's son, after all.

He'd stayed home from church last Sunday, too sick at heart to make himself show his face in public. Wyatt had already warned that he was not going to get away with that a second time. Since then, Ryder had done his best to carry on with life as normal, fearing that this awful struggle to simply put one foot in front of another *was* his new normal. Still, what choice did he have?

Lord, give me the strength to get over this, he prayed before forcing himself into a sitting position. Numbly, he swung his legs over the side of the bed, but then he dropped his head into his hands and struggled to think of something, anything, other than Jeri.

Strangely, his deepest regret was that he hadn't spoken to her that last night, a week ago now. After the newspaper had come out on Friday, he'd spent all his time digesting what had happened and planning what he was going to say to her. Though his family was precious to him, he'd nixed any birthday celebration. He just wasn't up to pretending to enjoy their good wishes. The speeches he'd imagined delivering to Jeri had run the gamut from raging to cold indifference, all designed to wound her and impress upon her how deeply she had wounded him. In the end, he hadn't even been able to look at her. His chief emotion now was a yawning sense of loss, a painful emptiness that he kept begging God to fill.

The support of friends had helped, at least with his fears of public rejection. Stark and Meri Burns had been the first to show up, voicing their support and concern.

"No one who knows you could believe that nonsense they printed," Meri insisted. "We've always understood how deeply you regret and grieve what happened."

Rex and Callie Billings had come over with a pro bono offer to sue the newspaper. Despite openly admitting that the chances of success were slim, Rex thought it might be possible to get a retraction and find out exactly who the anonymous source was. That person could then be sued for slander. Ryder had refused. Why drag the thing out publicly? Besides, little in the story could be proved an outright lie. He just didn't have the energy or inclination to fight this thing any longer. Obviously, Bryan's death was a tragedy that he would carry with him for the rest of his life. Perhaps that was just. Ryder didn't know, but God did, and He was Ryder's last refuge.

That being the case, he couldn't very well sit here

feeling sorry for himself when the hour for the worship service loomed. Besides, Dean and Ann Pryor had stated firmly that they would be waiting for him at the church door when he arrived. Time to tend the horses.

He rose and dressed in yesterday's clothes then went out to the barn. Over the past week, he'd gotten in the habit of skipping breakfast. His appetite had vanished, and it was all he could do to make himself choke down a few bites at lunch or dinner. Tending the horses had become a special kind of comfort to him. He'd spent long hours with them, saddling and riding at least one of the Loco Man herd every day and walking Jeri's remaining two. Wyatt had vowed to send her horses back to Stark, but then a deposit had shown up in the B and B account, enough to cover her room rent and the care of the horses for the rest of the month. The bank had informed them that refusing and returning the payment would require two weeks or more, so Wyatt had settled for blocking any further receipts.

Ryder was glad about that. Having Dovie and Betty around gave him a strange, hopeful comfort. He greeted them both daily with lavish affection and toyed with the idea of telling Jeri that she couldn't have them back. Of course, he'd have to call or text her to manage that, and he couldn't do that. Not yet.

After spending as much time with the horses as he dared, Ryder went back to the bunkhouse and got ready for church. When it was time to go, he opened the front door to find Wyatt standing there with a raised fist.

"Oh," his big brother said. "You're ready."

"Ready as I'll ever be," Ryder muttered, plopping his hat onto his head. Wyatt clapped him on the shoulder as they walked side by side to the carport. At the last moment, Ryder decided to take his own truck. Jake, who had brought Kathryn over to stay with Tina, argued briefly, but Ryder insisted. He was a grown man. He would stand on his own two feet even if that meant merely arriving alone to church.

Dean and Ann weren't waiting at the door as promised. Instead, despite the cold weather, they were standing in the parking lot. Wyatt and Jake and the boys pulled in right behind him, but the Pryors fixed their focus on Ryder and engulfed him with embraces as soon as he slid out onto the ground. A little embarrassed but also comforted, he walked toward the building in the center of a determined cadre of support, but when they got to the door, he asked Wyatt to hold up. Then Ryder stepped forward, pulled open that door and entered alone.

The pastor stood just inside. As the others piled up behind Ryder, letting cold air into the foyer, the pastor grasped his hand and slid an arm across his shoulders.

"Ryder, I had no idea what trauma you've been through with this Bryan Averrett tragedy. Please know that we will keep Bryan's family in our prayers and add you to each of them."

Stunned, all Ryder could do was stammer his thanks. Then Wes and Dr. Alice Shorter Billings embraced him. Others hurried to him with hugs and murmurs of comfort. Some had done no more than shake his hand in the past. Others had let a nod of acknowledgement suffice. Now they rushed to show their support. Despite feeling that much of this had been orchestrated by his friends, Ryder was more than grateful. Humbled almost to the point of tears, he silently accepted every greeting, his smile strained but his heart swelling.

Later he told himself that he couldn't expect the same treatment from those who had not sat in prayer meeting with him. He was wrong. Perhaps some did wonder privately if recklessness or irresponsibility on his part had killed Bryan, but once he started appearing in public again, people he barely knew came up to say how horrible they'd found the newspaper article to be and wish him well. Abe Tolly even called him.

"I never dreamed you were dealing with something like this, son. Don't let other people's envy get the better of you."

"Envy?"

"Sure. What else could be behind such scurrilous nonsense? Good-looking boy like you, with your skills and gentle nature, lesser folks are just going to naturally be jealous. Besides, that poor young man's own sister knows you didn't murder her brother. She so obviously loves you."

Ryder had no reply for that. For days, he'd let incriminating bits and pieces of their conversations and interactions float unchallenged through his mind. Jeri dropping that mineral block on his toes and delaying their progress on the range with accident after presumed accident… Jeri finding fault with every property Tolly had shown her, even though finding a place was her only stated reason for coming at all… Jeri pressing him for details about Bryan's death… So much that she had said and done now seemed like clear indications of her perfidy.

Ryder had paid no attention to Wyatt's misgivings about her or to Ox's warning that something didn't add up. The fact that Jeri had stopped him when he'd tried to tell her that he loved her and wanted to marry her now seemed particularly ominous.

After Abe Tolly's call, though, Ryder began to remember other things, like how she'd absolved him after she'd heard the full story of Bryan's death.

You're sensible and good.

She hadn't just helped Tina, she'd *offered* to help Tina, and she'd continued to show her concern. He remembered how she was with the boys and little Glory Pryor, and how she'd almost wept with delight and relief when he'd suggested moving her horses from Stark's to Loco Man. They'd worked so well together, he and Jeri, like a team of long standing. And what about the day she'd turned to him for comfort after burning all the bread and cheese in the house—a disaster stemming from nothing worse than a desire to help by making lunch? He recalled feeding her French fries and how she'd come so easily into his arms, the way she'd pressed against him and turned her lovely face up for his kiss, her hat dangling between his shoulder blades as she'd wrapped her arms around his neck.

The pain of loss swirled through him so heavily that he staggered beneath the weight of it. Shoving aside the memories, he searched for other things to think about. Horses. He sat and thought on that for a long time. Then he saddled up and took a ride around the property. The next day he did the same thing. On the third day, he asked his brothers to meet him at Jake's shop. When they were all gathered, he didn't beat around the bush.

"I want a quarter section of land for horses."

The moment they looked at each other, he knew they'd discussed this at some length, but he didn't give them time to accede or refuse. Instead, he stated, firmly, what he expected.

"I want it in my name."

"But you already own it with us," Wyatt objected. "That'll just make you personally responsible for the taxes on that part of the ranch."

"That's all right," Ryder insisted. "I want it in my name because I intend to build a house, and I don't want any guff from either of you about what I put on the property. Nags or thoroughbreds, it's my business."

"A house will require a mortgage," Wyatt pointed out, lifting a hand to the back of his neck.

"And?"

There went that look again. This time he saw some surprise and a bit of relief, maybe even a smattering of pride.

Jake cleared his throat, wiped the wrench in his left hand with the rag in his right and asked, "You sure a hundred and sixty acres is enough for what you have in mind?"

Ryder grinned. "It's a start. That's all I want right now."

"I'll speak to Rex about drawing up the papers," Wyatt said, and that was that.

On Friday, the *Tri-County Weekly* printed a retraction of sorts, quoting Jeri Bogman as saying that Ryder had been rightfully cleared of any and all responsibility in her brother's death. The article also stated that she, for one, bore him no ill will and knew how deeply he regretted the "accident." The Ardmore paper printed a short piece, also quoting her, in Monday's edition.

"My brother was more responsible for his death than anyone else," Jeri was quoted as saying. "I know how difficult that is for my mother to accept, but it's the truth."

That told Ryder the identity of the anonymous source, and he could only be thankful that he hadn't pursued a defamation suit. The woman had suffered more than enough. And so had Jeri.

I miss my brother especially.

What would have happened if she'd confessed right then that Bryan was her brother? They could have cleared the air, come to a complete understanding about Bryan's death. But then what? Ryder knew with shocking certainty that he wouldn't have had the courage to pursue her if he'd known she was related to Bryan. His own sense of guilt would have stopped him. Besides, she'd likely have left the ranch after learning the truth, and that would have been the end of it.

He'd have missed holding her and kissing her. They wouldn't have worked together for hours or sat together and talked and laughed. Fort Worth would never have happened, and he wouldn't have felt the bone-deep thrill of loving and wanting her, of knowing that she loved and wanted him.

A rush of gladness swept over him when he visualized how happy she'd been to see him there.

My boyfriend, she'd said, and he had been so pleased to hear it.

He remembered then how eager she'd been to see him after coming home from a rodeo, and how warmly she'd responded to his every touch. Other memories, suppressed until this moment, swirled around him.

I never thought I wouldn't want to leave you.

He saw her smile and the warmth in her eyes as she gazed up at him, felt her snuggle against his chest and rise up on tiptoe to bring her lips to his. He heard her promise to make it home in time for his birthday. And she had.

That brought thoughts of the gift he'd inadvertently stepped on and never opened. Kathryn had handed it to him a few days later. He'd tossed it onto the shelf in his living room, next to the photo of his parents and brothers, unopened.

Going to it now, he pulled away torn paper and broke the ribbon to remove the top of the flat, flimsy box. He brushed aside more paper and saw a hat pin affixed to a black-and-white bandanna. In silver script, the pin spelled out the words "Loco Man Ranch." Picking up the bandanna so he could release the pin, he saw more words embroidered near the hem in bright red thread.

"JERI'S COWBOY."

An identical bandanna beneath it read, "RYDER'S COWGIRL."

He ran his fingertip over the embroidery, coming to a conclusion that quieted something within him. She loved him. It hadn't been an act. Bryan Averrett's sister had loved him, at least for a time.

That didn't mean things could work out between them. He couldn't imagine how they might overcome the fact that he had, however inadvertently, been involved in her brother's death. And then there was the family. They were so angry on his behalf. But if she could forgive him for Bryan's death, surely he could forgive her for her deception.

Maybe she'd intended to hurt him somehow when she'd come there, but she'd mainly brought him joy. He knew they had to talk about that, but he wasn't ready. If he saw her now, he feared the pain would blossom again and he'd lash out. That wouldn't solve anything. Besides, his family wasn't likely to be amenable to the idea.

"You tell me when, Lord," he whispered, holding that bandanna in his hand.

Maybe the moment would never come, but he was willing to go there if that was where the Lord led him. Or he would be. Eventually. Meanwhile, she had two horses and some other stuff here. The tie was not entirely broken. Not yet.

He released the pin from the bandanna. The latter he tucked back into the box, but he connected the pin to his dress hat.

No, the tie was not broken.

Only his heart.

And he was beginning to think he might live through that, after all.

Chapter Fifteen

She hadn't won a race in weeks. Thankfully, she'd managed—barely—to finish in the money a couple times. It was enough to pay her expenses, so Jeri kept on keeping on. It was tough, though. She'd spent every night in her trailer since leaving Loco Man Ranch, not that she slept much. She kept seeing Ryder's back and bowed head at the table there in the ranch house kitchen and his big, booted feet as he'd walked past her with neither word nor glance.

About all she could logically do was call the newspapers in Oklahoma that had printed her mother's lies and set the record straight. She couldn't bring herself to go back to the ranch to pick up her horses or the personal things she'd left behind, so she'd arranged payment for their upkeep. Thankfully, Tina had swiped her debit card when she'd first checked in.

Meanwhile, Jeri ached for home and those she'd left there.

It wasn't just Ryder whom she missed, though he was by far the one she missed the most. She couldn't help worrying about Tina or thinking of the boys and Kathryn, whom she admired more than the woman could know. She even missed Jake's teasing and Wyatt's protective, big-brother attitude. She longed for her bed and boisterous meals at the family table and, most of all, those quite moments of connectivity that she'd found with Ryder.

Her mother called, raving, when she found out that Jeri had given her own interview to the papers. "How dare you?" she demanded. "How dare you let him off the hook like that? He killed your brother!"

"Bryan killed himself, Mom. I know it wasn't intentional, but he was more responsible than Ryder, and you know it. You have the coroner's report that says Bryan was abusing anabolic steroids, as well as the unedited video of what happened."

"Bryan was only twenty-one!" Dena raged, tacitly confirming Jeri's suspicions about the report and video being in Dena's possession the whole time. "Where do you think he got those steroids? He didn't find them on the street!"

"He didn't get them from Ryder," Jeri stated firmly. "You know Ryder wasn't using because you have that report, too."

Dena didn't deny it. "So what? That just means he knew how bad those drugs are. It doesn't mean he wasn't selling them!"

"Stop grasping at straws, Mom. Bryan is gone, and no one is more responsible for his death than he is. You have to let it go."

"How can you do this to me? How can you do this to your brother?"

"I'm not doing anything to either of you," Jeri replied softly. "I'm just stating the facts, and I don't believe Bryan would condemn me for that."

"Well, I do!" Dena screamed, breaking the connection.

After that, Jeri had nothing left but prayer and tears. She basically divided her free time between the two.

Valentine's Day was tough, so tough she pretended to receive phone calls from Ryder to keep Lacy from knowing how badly she'd blown it with him. They met in New Mexico, and when Lacy remarked how sad Jeri seemed to be, she blamed it on missing Ryder, which was entirely true. Thankfully, Lacy and Ox were in contact only sporadically and apparently he'd said nothing about the situation with Ryder, which made Jeri wonder if Ox even knew.

On a dreary Wednesday evening in Idaho, Jeri pulled over on impulse just outside of Boise to attend prayer meeting at a local church with a sign out front proclaiming that all were welcome. Afterward, she found herself tearfully pouring out her heart to the pastor and his wife, explaining her brother's death and her mother's angry refusal to accept the truth of the situation. They'd promised to pray for everyone concerned. The following Sunday, at the Cowboy Church service on the rodeo grounds, Jeri requested prayer again. She didn't go into detail, but a group of cowboys and cowgirls surrounded her to pray, and then a funny thing began to happen.

Happy memories of her brother began to infiltrate her thoughts. She began to pray that her mother might receive them also and come to peace with his death enough to appreciate what they'd shared of his life. She prayed, too, for the rest of the Smith family, even Tina's unborn babies. Images of Ryder waiting for her when she pulled into the Loco Man compound after driving all day to get there began to replace those last haunting images of his disappointment in her. She saw herself opening the trailer door again to find him standing there with Ox and felt the chuckle in his chest as he'd held her close while she bawled about burning all those grilled cheese sandwiches. She relived his every kiss with deep gratitude and abiding joy. And she came to a conclusion.

He'd loved her. He had loved her as no one else ever had or ever could, and she had only herself to blame for killing that love. Still, it had been hers for a while, a sweet, sweet while.

She journeyed on, all the way to the west coast. Then, out of the blue, she received a text from Ryder on the last Friday of February.

Come home.

Not "Come and get your horses," or even "Come back to the ranch." All he wrote was Come home.

With tears dripping from her eyes and hope building in her chest, she replied, Leaving CA Sun Mar 1.

She heard nothing more from him, but she had her best race to date on Leap Day, February 29, and on Sunday she walked away with the grand prize money. She left that night for Oklahoma, timing her arrival so that she pulled into the compound at Loco Man Ranch midafternoon on Tuesday, March 3. No one waited for her, but just arriving was like balm to her soul. She pulled the rig to a stop in front of the barn and walked to the house without her hat or jacket, inhaling the clean, crisp air and the silence. Bracing herself for an awkward greeting, she climbed the steps to the back stoop and tapped on the door.

After several minutes, she tapped again. Minutes after that, she opened the door and stuck her head inside, voicing a timid, "Hello?"

All she heard in reply was a muffled cry and an anxious voice saying, "Dr. Alice is in Ringling, and the ambulance is twenty minutes out."

That sounded like Kathryn, trying to keep her voice low, but Jeri caught the edge of panic. Ryder appeared at the end of the hallway, shoving his hands through his hair and twisting them about in consternation. He didn't see Jeri, not even when she walked through the door and closed it behind her.

"We'll have to put her in the truck and meet them on the way," he decided.

Kathryn joined him then. "What if she delivers before you reach them?"

He shook his head. "I don't know, but her water broke, so we have to do something. Now."

"Call Stark Burns," Jeri blurted.

They both jerked around to gape at her.

"He can help. He's made hundreds of deliveries."

Still, they just stared at her.

"He's better than nothing!"

Ryder plucked his phone out of his pocket and made the call, repeating Stark's instructions for Kathryn and Jeri to hear. "Towels. Gloves. Antiseptic. Suture thread? No, he's got that."

"I've got sterile gloves and antiseptic in my first aid kit," Jeri said, yanking open the door again and bolting for the truck.

She heard Tina scream before she got back to the

house. It was too late for Stark or anyone else to be of help. It was up to her now. Running for the bedroom, she bawled, "Gimme a clean shirt! Now!"

Someone dropped a white, long-sleeved shirt in front of her face as she fell to her knees beside the bed, issuing orders.

"Turn her! The footboard's in the way."

While Jeri stuffed her arms into the sleeves of the shirt and someone tugged it up onto her shoulders, backward so that it opened behind her, Wyatt appeared on the other side of the bed. Leaning one knee on the mattress, he grasped Tina under both arms and hauled her around so that she lay sideways on the wide bed. Jeri threw back the twisted top sheet, appalled at the mess, but Kathryn stepped forward and quickly helped her remove the necessary clothing and slid a clean towel into place. Tina screamed again. Jeri barely had time to rip open the package and pull on the gloves before the first baby appeared. He slid into her hands, tiny and silent.

"Boy!" Kathryn reported triumphantly. "Lots of black hair."

He wasn't moving at all, so Jeri did the only thing she could think of—what she'd always done for newly born puppies, kittens, foals and other animals. She grabbed a towel from the folded stack that had appeared on the foot of the bed and began rubbing vigorously. Within moments the baby spit up pinkish fluid and started to wail, waving his tiny hands and arms angrily. Wyatt laughed, tears coursing down his face.

"Is he all right?" Tina queried tremulously.

"He's perfect," Jeri said, laying him carefully on the pillow that Kathryn moved next to Tina. "Small but perfect."

She didn't know what to do next. She'd watched many a litter being delivered, but human beings were in a category by themselves, and there was another waiting to make an entrance. Should she cut the cord now or wait? Before she had a chance to decide how to proceed, Stark showed up, breathless and with a medical kit in tow.

"Thank God," Jeri exclaimed, but he didn't make it around the foot of the bed before Tina stopped him.

"No! I don't want him doing this. Or any of the men. It's embarrassing enough as it is!"

Jeri looked up at Stark beseechingly. He had frozen in place, but now he carefully set the kit on the corner of the bed. He opened it, laying out several sterile packets before lifting his hands and backing away.

"I—I'm not sure exactly how to—"

That was all she got out before Tina pressed the soles of her feet into the mattress, growled deep in her throat like a mother bear and yelled in pain. Jeri had to help the second little guy, who came into the world howling before he was even fully born, but Stark talked her through it, and all that followed, from a safe distance. She was trembling and Tina was sobbing with relief and delight by the time Jeri laid the second twin, swaddled in towels, in his mother's arms. The ambulance siren was clearly audible even before then.

Looking up at her, Wyatt nodded. "Thank God you're here."

Jeri could do no more than nod back. She stripped off the gloves, turning them wrong side out, and pulled away the shirt, which she doubted anyone would want to rescue. Dropping the lot where she stood, she wobbled toward the door. Stark clapped her on the shoulder as she passed into the hallway.

"Good work."

And then there was Ryder, his dark gaze searching hers. She burst into tears, partly from anxiety, partly from relief, partly from the sheer joy of seeing him again. To her everlasting delight, he smiled, and then he pulled her into his arms. She collapsed against his chest, sobbing.

Without even a thought, her words came pouring out. "I love you. I love you. Please, please, if you never believe anything else, believe that."

He curled a finger beneath her chin and turned her face up. "I love you, too."

Dumbstruck, she could do nothing more than gape at him for a long moment. Then he cupped a big hand around the curve of her jaw as if she was the most precious thing in the world. She launched herself upward, bringing her lips to his.

Jake gently nudged them aside a few moments later, making way for the EMTs and the gurney they had wheeled through the kitchen. Jeri and Ryder stood wrapped in each other's arms while the gurney disappeared into the bedroom then reappeared some minutes later, bearing a very composed Tina and the smaller of the twins. Wyatt followed with the other baby in his arms. Tina reached out a hand toward Jeri, and the gurney paused.

"Thank you. And welcome back."

Jeri nodded and started to cry again. The gurney moved on. Wyatt appeared. He pulled back the towel to show Ryder his nephew. Ryder kept Jeri close as he peered at the newborn.

"Wow. I mean… Wow."

Grinning, Wyatt carried the infant out to the waiting

ambulance. Jake and Kathryn followed them with coats, gloves and hats. Ryder and Jeri stayed where they were, holding each other, until Jake and Kathryn returned.

"The EMTs say everyone should be fine," Jake announced. "The babies are small, but they're breathing on their own. We're going to follow Wyatt and the ambulance to the hospital. Would you mind trading trucks with me and bringing the boys? That way I won't have to move car seats."

Ryder looked at Jeri.

"I need to unload my horses."

"We'll take care of the boys here," Ryder decided, tossing Jake his keys. "But take my truck anyway, just in case. Let us know what the doctors say."

Jake dropped his own keys on the table beside the door, snapped a little salute and started to follow Kathryn out the door once more, but then he paused and looked back.

"Welcome home, Jeri."

"Thank you," she choked out.

"There's one thing about us Smith men," Jake added. "We attract the most remarkable women." With that, he stepped out and pulled the door closed behind him.

"That's the truth," Ryder muttered.

Jeri immediately began apologizing. "Ryder, I'm so sorry for not telling you the whole truth immediately."

"I know. I understand why you didn't, and I'm willing to forgive you and move past it all. But I have a few conditions, so you'd better listen."

"Whatever you say."

"This all happened way too fast, but I'm not putting up with any long-drawn-out engagement. I intend to go with you the next time you leave here. Do you understand me?"

Elated, Jeri nodded. "I'll marry you tomorrow if you want. There's just one thing."

"What's that?"

"My mother hates you. I've tried to reason with her, but she just won't or can't hear me."

Sighing, Ryder pulled Jeri against his chest again. "Poor woman. We'll have to pray on that. But it's not her I'm worried about. You're all I want. All I need. So, if you can't truly forgive me for what happened to Bryan, tell me now."

"There's nothing to forgive," Jeri exclaimed, pulling back far enough to look up at him. "I can't even think of it like that. In some ways, it's almost as if…as if Bryan's brought us together."

"That's a beautiful way to think about it," Ryder murmured, staring past her. Suddenly, he smiled and said, "I sure wish he was here."

"Me, too."

Locking his arms around her, Ryder twitched an eyebrow. "There's something else you should know. I've got a quarter section of my own now, and I'm getting ready to build a house on it."

"A house!"

He nodded. "A hundred and sixty acres doesn't sound like much, but Abe says there's a forty-acre parcel right on our fence line that we ought to be able to pick up cheap."

We.

That word sounded like her every dream come true. With room to grow.

"I love you, Ryder Smith," she whispered. "From now on, wherever you are, that's my home."

"Sounds perfect to me."

Suddenly, a picture of her brother flashed before her mind's eye. The very last time she'd seen him, he'd been laughing at her concerns. His car sat packed behind him, and he'd been about to head out for Houston, excited and full of life.

"I love you, bro. I mean, sis. Why'd Mom give you a guy's name, anyway? Never mind. You just go and do your thing and don't worry about me. Okay?"

"Okay," she whispered.

Then she closed her eyes and silently thanked God, Who had obviously been at work this whole time to bring her and Ryder together. In so doing, He had even given meaning to her brother's death.

She had come for revenge.

And would stay for love.

* * * * *

If you loved this story,
check out the other books from
Arlene James's miniseries
Three Brothers Ranch

The Rancher's Answered Prayer
Rancher to the Rescue

Or pick up these other stories of ranch life
from the author's previous miniseries
The Prodigal Ranch

The Rancher's Homecoming
Her Single Dad Hero
Her Cowboy Boss

Available now from Love Inspired!

Find more great reads at www.LoveInspired.com

Dear Reader,

God can bless us even through tragedy.

When I first experienced the tragic death of a young person, just being told that God could and would bless those who suffered that loss infuriated me. More than forty years later, I know beyond a shadow of a doubt that the same God Who allows tragedy can and will bless His children in and through that same tragedy. Sometimes we're too broken to realize we've been blessed. Sometimes we're too angry. Sometimes we haven't forgiven, and sometimes that includes not forgiving ourselves. That's exactly the predicament Ryder and Jeri are in at the beginning of this story.

I'm so happy to be able to give Ryder and Jeri the blessings of forgiveness, peace and love, but I realize that many others touched by tragedy, like Jeri's mother, are unable to receive the blessings granted to them. My prayers are with them—and with you, my readers.

God bless. Always,

Arlene James

Get 4 FREE REWARDS!

We'll send you 2 FREE Books plus 2 FREE Mystery Gifts.

Love Inspired® books feature contemporary inspirational romances with Christian characters facing the challenges of life and love.

FREE Value Over **$20**

YES! Please send me 2 FREE Love Inspired® Romance novels and my 2 FREE mystery gifts (gifts are worth about $10 retail). After receiving them, if I don't wish to receive any more books, I can return the shipping statement marked "cancel." If I don't cancel, I will receive 6 brand-new novels every month and be billed just $5.24 for the regular-print edition or $5.74 each for the larger-print edition in the U.S., or $5.74 each for the regular-print edition or $6.24 each for the larger-print edition in Canada. That's a savings of at least 13% off the cover price. It's quite a bargain! Shipping and handling is just 50¢ per book in the U.S. and 75¢ per book in Canada.* I understand that accepting the 2 free books and gifts places me under no obligation to buy anything. I can always return a shipment and cancel at any time. The free books and gifts are mine to keep no matter what I decide.

Choose one: ☐ **Love Inspired® Romance Regular-Print**
(105/305 IDN GMY4)   ☐ **Love Inspired® Romance Larger-Print**
(122/322 IDN GMY4)

Name (please print)

Address   Apt. #

City   State/Province   Zip/Postal Code

Mail to the **Reader Service:**
IN U.S.A.: P.O. Box 1341, Buffalo, NY 14240-8531
IN CANADA: P.O. Box 603, Fort Erie, Ontario L2A 5X3

Want to try 2 free books from another series? Call 1-800-873-8635 or visit www.ReaderService.com.

---

*Terms and prices subject to change without notice. Prices do not include sales taxes, which will be charged (if applicable) based on your state or country of residence. Canadian residents will be charged applicable taxes. Offer not valid in Quebec. This offer is limited to one order per household. Books received may not be as shown. Not valid for current subscribers to Love Inspired Romance books. All orders subject to approval. Credit or debit balances in a customer's account(s) may be offset by any other outstanding balance owed by or to the customer. Please allow 4 to 6 weeks for delivery. Offer available while quantities last.

Your Privacy—The Reader Service is committed to protecting your privacy. Our Privacy Policy is available online at www.ReaderService.com or upon request from the Reader Service. We make a portion of our mailing list available to reputable third parties that offer products we believe may interest you. If you prefer that we not exchange your name with third parties, or if you wish to clarify or modify your communication preferences, please visit us at www.ReaderService.com/consumerchoice or write to us at Reader Service Preference Service, P.O. Box 9062, Buffalo, NY 14240-9062. Include your complete name and address.

LI19R2

Yasmin shifted on the glider, set it rocking with one foot and tucked the other foot up under her. The air was cooling now, a slight breeze bringing the fragrance of oleander flowers. It seemed only natural for Liam to shuffle closer on the glider. To let his arm curve around her shoulders.

Yasmin's breath whooshed out of her. Talking with Liam about her brother had made her feel vulnerable, but also relieved. Less alone. She remembered when she could share anything with Liam and he would always have her back. Such a wonderful feeling, especially after her brother had stopped being able to be that rock and that support to her.

Now Liam turned to meet her gaze head-on. His hand rose to brush back a curl that had escaped her ponytail. "I like your hairstyle," he said unexpectedly, his voice a tone deeper than usual. "Reminds me of the old days, when we were in school."

"In other words, I look like a kid?" Her words came out breathy, and she couldn't take her eyes off him.

Slowly, Liam shook his head. "Oh, no, Yasmin. You don't look like a kid at all." His eyes flickered down to her mouth, then back to her eyes.

Yasmin's heart fluttered like a terrified bird. Her stomach, her chest, all that was inside her felt squeezed by warm hands, melting.

How she wanted this. This opportunity to talk to Liam in a low, intimate voice. To feel that sense of promise, that there was something happy and bright in their future together.

She tried to grasp on to the reasons why this couldn't happen. How she didn't dare to have children, because the risk of them developing a mental illness was so high. Not only because of Josiah, although that was the main thing, of course. But also because of her mother's issues.

As if all of that wasn't enough, Yasmin knew she wasn't past the safe age herself. What if she got into a relationship and then started having delusions and hearing voices?

It was hard enough taking care of her brother, her blood relative. She owed him and bore the burden gladly. But she couldn't expect a romantic partner to do the same for her, wouldn't want someone to.

Wouldn't want Liam to.

If she let things go where they were headed right now, if she let him kiss her, she wasn't sure she would have the strength to push him away again. Doing it once had nearly killed her. Maybe she could be strong enough, but only if she put an end to this before getting closer. "I think we should go."

His head tilted to one side, his eyes steady on her. "Do you really think so?"

She hesitated, clung for just a moment to the possibility of not being the responsible one, the caretaker, the one who took charge of things and tried to make everything work out. She could let herself do what she wanted to do every now and then, couldn't she? She could be spontaneous, go with her emotions, her heart.

But no. Her duty was clear. Her life was about taking care of her family, not about indulging in something pleasurable for now, but ultimately dangerous to someone she cared about. Liam was too good of a man, had suffered too many of life's blows already, to be shackled with Yasmin's issues. "Yes," she said firmly. "I really think so."

Don't miss Lee Tobin McClain's
Low Country Dreams, *available June 2019*
wherever Harlequin® books and ebooks are sold.

www.Harlequin.com

PHLTMEXP0619

Looking for inspiration in tales of hope, faith and heartfelt romance?

Check out **Love Inspired**® and **Love Inspired**® **Suspense** books!

New books available every month!
